SWITCH BACK

JACK LIVELY

GENERAL PROJECTS

To Madam Roja and her piano.

SWITCH BACK

Black vultures swept out of the big desert sky. The birds had been cruising for a few minutes. When they came down, I knew that something out there was dead.

I was about a half mile away, walking off track, boots crunching on rocks and the hard plants that grow there. The buzzards were black specks in the sky. It was hot, maybe the hottest day of the year. I was in Big Bend National Park, Texas, a stone's throw from the Mexican border. It took me around ten minutes to get into the hills. I was sweating hard by the time I climbed up the valley to a hillside pocked with shaded crevices.

I found the body wedged between boulders at the entrance to a shallow overhang. There were around two dozen buzzards on the corpse. The birds scattered when I approached, but stuck around, waiting for the chance to get back in there.

The dead guy had survived into his thirties. It looked as though death had come as a major surprise. His mouth was gaping, the eyes open wide. The color had gone out of him already, so his skin was pasty and yellow. Flies buzzed around an exposed wound on his head and in and out of his mouth and nostrils, settling down on his eyeballs.

I squatted down to inspect the wound.

The skull was fractured and the broken bone was pushed inward. But the broken off pieces had fragmented after the first impact, which meant repeated blows. This was not an accidental death. The guy had not fallen onto his head from a cliff. Neither had he been pushed out of an airplane. No giant had picked him up and flung him down to earth. He had been murdered. Recently. The blood was sticky, not yet dry. Straight black hair was still plastered to his head with sweat. The buzzards had only just begun to feed.

A couple of feet away from the body was a black baseball cap with an embroidered Chihuahua on the front. I figured it had gotten knocked off when his skull was caved in by someone holding the bloodied, grapefruit-sized rock at rest near the body. I looked at the murder weapon and pictured the hand that had held it. It occurred to me that the person to whom that hand belonged was still around. So, I stood up straight, took a good look around and called out, "Hello," and then, "Hola." But the only thing I got in return was my own voice, echoed back by the stubborn hillside.

∼

HIKING under the Texas sun had not been a pre-meditated plan, like a vacation or a retreat. It had happened by way of several interconnected events and personalities.

I had been out on Vancouver Island for a couple of weeks, helping Steve Bell harvest Gooseneck barnacles off rocks for the Japanese buyers. A Gooseneck barnacle is a type of seafood, like a clam or lobster, but attached to rocks. Americans don't eat many of them. We think they look alien, not like good eating. But, the folks in Japan, Spain, and Portugal think of them as very good eating. What's more, they have eaten up their own supply. Steve had cottoned on to this, and set himself up as an exporter. Steve had needed help with his new venture, so I figured helping him was the right thing to do.

Now he was doing alright. Gooseneck barnacles are seriously hard to get, and seriously expensive. Good for Steve, okay for me. Steve's business had picked up, and I was glad to help a friend. On top of that, he paid me. The water off Vancouver Island is cold all year round, and the sea spray in your face is bracing. In the beginning there had been a Swedish girl involved. But by the time Steve had come around to mentioning the situation with Mallory, the Swedish girl was gone.

We were in the truck driving back from the spot. Steve was never a big talker, and I'm fine with that. So, it was really out of nowhere that Steve said, "You heard about Mallory, right?"

I had not heard about anything, or spoken to anyone. Hadn't even thought about Mallory in years. The last time I'd seen her was in Northeast Syria, through a swirling storm of rotor dust as she lifted the Pave Hawk helicopter out of a hot landing zone. Mallory had glanced at me, making eye contact. My team was already taking fire. Thirty seconds later the chopper was out of sight and out of mind.

"No Steve, I didn't hear about Mallory. What about her?"

Steve had been driving along, quietly looking through the windshield at the road, watching it curve along the jagged coastline. He said, "Brain cancer. Three months, max. She asked about you. That was about a month and a half ago."

The first thing that came to mind was the meaning of her name, Mallory, which means *unfortunate* in French. My mother was born in France, and I speak the language.

"Sorry to hear that."

"Yeah. It sucks."

"How's she taking it?"

Steve hadn't actually spoken to Mallory, or seen her in person. The conversation had been conducted over the internet, in something called a group chat, apparently by text message, with the use of thumbs. He said, "I don't know. How does anyone take that? I guess badly, but bravely."

"I guess so, knowing Mallory."

Mallory had been a combat search and rescue pilot attached to the 322nd Special Tactics Squadron, which was me and Steve and a bunch of other operators. She was brave, that was for damn sure. It didn't take long for me to process the fact that she had terminal cancer and wanted to see me. If Mallory wanted to see me, I was going to show up. Period.

I packed my bag that night and hit the road early the next morning. Flew from Vancouver to San Antonio via Los

Angeles. From San Antonio, I picked up a blue Ford rental car for the five-hour drive west to Twin Forks, Mallory's home town. It was after midnight by the time I got in to Twin Forks. The town was an eerie bunch of lights in a featureless desert night with no moon. I found a spot to pull off the road, racked the seat back, and closed my eyes.

I woke hungry and cramped from sitting in the Ford rental. I pulled the car around and got back on the main road through town. Sign said, Gas and Food, a happy combination, in my mind. I mentally added the word 'coffee.' The gas station had a single pump out front, two garage doors on the south side, and a big picture window on the north. Inside the picture window, I saw a counter with stools, a grill, and three deuces running along the south wall. I opened the door, disturbing a little bell, which rattled softly.

A guy sat in front of a cash register, with a pencil and a sudoku book. He looked up at me when I walked in. "Food or gas?"

"Food."

"Take a seat."

The counter was five stools across, with ample space between seats. Each stool with its fair share of elbow room. The fifth stool was taken by a big guy wearing an apron. He had an empty plate in front of him smeared with grease and a ceramic cup with a lone star logo. I took the second stool in the row. The guy slowly pushed his cup and plate across the counter, slid off the stool, and came around to the grill side, like he was switching roles. He picked up the mug and took a sip, looking at me over the rim.

"What'll you have there, buddy?"

"Two eggs, bacon, toast, coffee."

"Want chorizo with that?"

"Great idea."

"Beans?"

"Sure."

"White, whole wheat, or tortilla?"

"Whole wheat."

"How you like your coffee?"

"Black."

"You got it."

The cook worked the grill with well-rehearsed smooth movements. He handled the tools of his trade like they were old friends. The coffee was fresh. All was good. I was halfway through breakfast, and enjoying it, when the door opened. This time the bell did not tinkle softly, it clanged violently.

The guy at the register said, "Easy partner."

The new guy ignored him, came over and took the first stool, to my left. The new guy was around five nine, weighed about two-twenty. Big guy, horizontally speaking. He wore cargo shorts and a red polo shirt with a white logo at the breast. It said Dale's Oilfield Supply. He wore his hair long under a baseball hat. The new guy was giving off a whole lot of nervous energy, like what you might see with a sick animal.

The cook knew him. "What'll it be. Caleb?"

Caleb shoved his hand into one of the cargo pockets and pulled out a handful of change. He carefully spilled it on the counter and picked out the quarters.

"What can I get for two fifty?"

The cook said, "I'll do you a breakfast burrito, beans, egg and cheese, no bacon."

"Jesus Christ. How much for the bacon?"

"Dollar for meat."

Caleb looked at me. His face was red and puffy. He had two tears tattooed under his left eye.

He said, "Dollar for the meat," and looked back at the cook. "Dale fired me just now. I don't have the dollar. Can you do it for fifty cents?"

The cook shook his head, and looked out the window. The guy at the register made some marks in the sudoku book with his pencil. I pulled two dollars out of my pocket and slid them across the counter.

I said, "For the meat, and the coffee."

The guy called Caleb looked up at me again. "Man, I really appreciate that." He pushed the money across the counter to the cook. "See that? I'll take bacon and sausage on that burrito."

The cook said, "No coffee?"

"I don't drink coffee." Caleb turned to me. "Can't do caffeine, it interferes with my meds." He jerked his head at the cook, and raised his voice. "Not that I took my goddamned meds this morning either, but fuck it."

The cook started preparing the food. He said, "So what happens if you drink coffee with the medication, Caleb? You get dumber than you already are?"

Caleb shifted uncomfortably on the stool. "There's always some goddamned thing, either you can't take caffeine with the pills, or you can't *not* take the pills. It's like, what the hell *can* you do?"

The cook spooned a knob of lard onto the hot grill, it sizzled up immediately. He spread the grease out with his spatula, broke a couple of eggs onto the lubed-up steel surface. He bent down and took four slices of bacon and a sausage patty from an under-the-counter fridge. Laid them on the hot metal, which was beginning to smoke and sizzle with various animal fats mixing together with heat.

He wiped the spatula on a clean kitchen cloth. "So, why'd Dale fire you, Caleb?"

"For not showing up the last four days."

"So what, you show up today expecting to work after not showing up the last four days, and you're surprised that Dale fired you?"

"Something like that."

The cook shook his head. "I would not go blaming Dale for your problems, Caleb. Blame someone else."

"Yeah, like who?"

"Like maybe yourself?"

The eggs were almost done. The beans were sizzling quietly in a corner of the grill the cook had dialed down some. Two slices of cheese went on top of the eggs and started to wilt.

The cook said, "Ketchup, hot sauce?"

"Yup."

"Take out, eat in?"

Caleb said, "To go, I guess."

The cook shook salt and pepper over the eggs. Scraped everything into a rectangular shape. Two squeeze bottles emitted thin streams of red sauce. Then, he scooped all of that onto a big flour tortilla. He folded in the sides, then expertly rolled the burrito into a double sheet of waxed paper and foil, paired it with a napkin, and handed the hot fragrant bundle over to Caleb.

"So what're you going to do, now that you don't have a job anymore? Gonna tell your mom?"

Caleb took the burrito from him, and swiveled off the stool. He said, "I don't know. Guess I'll eat breakfast, then go shoot something or someone. I don't know." Caleb came down off the stool and started for the door. As he left, he flung back a loud comment. "Y'all have a nice life, you hear? You are alright by me. The rest of the world can go the fuck to hell." The door clanged shut.

The guy at the register looked back down at his sudoku. The cook said, "Hope I never see that loser again." He looked at me. "I guess you don't know him. If you did, you wouldn't have been so generous."

I watched out the window as Caleb hunched his big frame and squeezed into a beat-up old Honda. The car sputtered to life and belched smoke. Caleb was absorbed in unwrapping the burrito. He tore it open with his teeth, and spit paper and foil onto the passenger seat. Then, he took a large bite.

The guy at the register looked up at me, saw me looking. He dropped his head again to his puzzle. The Honda started rolling slowly across the gas station lot, toward the road. I could see Caleb's jaw chewing through the open driver's side window.

MALLORY'S PLACE was a ranch outside of town.

Took twenty minutes just to drive the rocky track from Texas route 117 to the ranch house, a low slung, single story classic built out of limestone and wood. The house was set on a wide driveway, with horse stables on one side, and a large fenced area for them to run. The fenced area was empty; I figured the horses were inside, protected from the swelling heat. A 1980s Ford Bronco was parked by the side of the house.

Mallory was at the door when I swung the car in. She was a slender woman in her thirties.

She looked good for someone who was scheduled to die, even with a bald head marked by an L shaped scar over her left ear. She hugged me hard and quick, and said, "Great to see you."

"Here I am."

She stood there in the doorway looking at me. Mallory cracked a smile. "Tom Keeler, how many times have I saved your ass?"

"Too many to count. These things we do . . ."

She shook her head. "Can't even save my own ass now."

"What I heard."

"Yeah. Fuck it, that's life."

"Looks that way."

Some people get torn up about the big changes in life, like death, babies, careers, relationships, and stock market crashes. I don't, and never have. People come to expect continuity. Like everything's going to settle at some point and just stay the same forever. But, as far as I can see, it doesn't work like that. Life and the universe follow no fixed rules whatsoever, except maybe gravity, in a relative way. You can never really know, and nothing ever stays the same. Nor would anyone want things to stay the same, not really, not when you take hopes and aspirations into account.

Mallory squinted into the hills. It was already hot out. She stepped back and let me into the house. Since we'd had plenty of time to jaw about this and that on deployment, I had heard about the house. The ranch had been in her family since the days when Texas had been its own republic. The house was built back then.

The entrance opened into a wide living area with low settees and a fireplace. The kitchen was just the other side of a countertop with bar stools tucked under. Mallory's dad stood up from the counter and came over to greet me. He was a rangy looking old guy with a bushy white mustache. I knew about him too. He'd been with the 101st Airborne in Vietnam, one of the long-range patrol units famous for unusually high body counts.

He shook my hand and put a cup of coffee in it. "Call me Dave."

I said, "Tom Keeler."

Dave went around to the kitchen and started whipping up eggs with beans and tortillas. I said nothing about my previous breakfast. Mallory excused herself. Dave followed her with his eyes, then swiveled them at me.

He said, "Good of you to come down."

"Thanks for having me."

"I'll give you the skinny while Mal's doing whatever she's doing." He looked over at me. I nodded to him. "Okay, so it's terminal. That's the first thing. There's no hope, no way, tumor is growing and there's not a damn thing anyone can do about it."

"That's what I heard."

He said, "Doctors say it could be a week, could be a day, it could be a month, but no way it's going to be more than a month, because that tumor is just squeezing its way into her brain."

"Is she in pain?"

"Bad headaches, drowsiness, all of it."

"Medication?"

He said, "She won't take the pills, unless the headaches get too bad, then she just takes a couple of aspirin. Tough kid. She's refusing to be hospitalized too."

I said nothing.

Dave continued. "So, we've already been cried out. No tears left anymore, that lake is dry. The only way forward is to accept it, let it happen."

"How's she doing, accepting it?"

"She's hanging tough, Keeler. I tell you something, you got to put your mind on a whole new level just to get a handle on that one, accepting that Mallory's going to be gone and dead, sooner rather than later."

I said nothing.

"She's doing better than me. I'll tell you that."

When Mallory came back, she sat down at the counter next to me and put an arm on my shoulder.

"Freak you out to see me like this?"

"It's what it is."

She said, "It's death. We've seen it before, a lot of it. Dad too."

"Scar looks impressive."

She traced the L shape above her ear. "They opened up my head with a saw, and scooped shit out of my brain, then they closed my head back up. Amazing."

"I'm guessing you weren't around for that one."

"Physically present, mentally AWOL."

Dave served up breakfast. We ate without speaking. My second breakfast. I figured something must be right, if my appetite was that good.

Dave asked, "How long you plan on staying, Keeler?"

"No plans, Dave. I'm here to help out if I can."

He nodded. Mallory looked at me, her eyes twinkled. "You can help us dig the grave. I'm going to be buried right here on the ranch, already picked out the spot."

I said, "Where's the spot?"

She pointed through a set of glass doors to a stand of oaks just beneath rolling hills, other side of the horse pen. "Under one of those trees."

The oak trees were widely spaced, and old. Thick trunks branched off low into powerful boughs. The curves were graceful.

I said, "That's a hell of a spot."

We did not get to talk much more than that however, because the two of them needed to go to the hospital for brain scans. Not that there was any hope, the results had already come in. Terminal, no doubt about it. Maybe a month, maybe a week, maybe a day. But still, the doctors at the Veteran Affairs medical center wanted the extra tests, for their statistical records, to help them more accurately predict tumor growth and the various complicated biological responses. So, Mallory and her dad were okay with getting tested again, if it could help out in the future. The VA medical center was over in Big Springs, about 200 miles away, a three hour trip.

They figured they would drive up there, get her scanned, eat lunch, and drive back in time for a late supper. Mallory estimated eight o'clock. Dave did a mental calculation and said, "More like eight fifteen, if the VA people are on schedule." Mallory wrote her mobile phone number on a post-it note and stuck it on the counter. I memorized the number.

She said, "Call me if anything happens."

I said, "Nothing's going to happen."

In the meantime, I was welcome to the fridge and the TV.

But I don't watch TV much, and I had just eaten two breakfasts. Plus, after traveling the best part of twenty-four hours just to get here, and sleeping all cramped up in the car, I felt like stretching my legs and getting some exercise. Which is how I ended up hiking into the Chisos mountains on the hottest day of the hottest month of the hottest year anyone could remember.

THE BODY WAS HALF in the shade, and half out. Hard sunlight clipped the dead guy at the waist. A vulture scooted in and took a peck on the guy's head wound. I figured I would let them have him.

I called out once more, "Hola." And got nothing back, except for echoes of my own voice, fading off like skimming stones into the desert. The guy did not look at rest. He looked dead. Flies were swarming the blood. The overhang was about halfway up the ravine, leading to a high ridge. I figured I could get up there and have a vantage point.

I got around ten yards up the slope when my peripheral vision clocked the girl.

She was hiding in a shady hole, screened by a large boulder. When I came around, I saw her, leaned back against the rocks and pointing a pistol at me. The gun was a Glock 19, and the girl's hands were steady, eyes wary. Her face was scratched up, as if she had been through thick brush during the crossing. She had an open cut and bruising on the right cheek below her eye. On top of that, she had a swollen lip. Her face and clothes were filthy with mud, dust, and dried blood. She looked like she had been through a lot.

I said, "I just lost a bet with myself. I'd been convinced that there was no armed person around. And here you are."

She wasn't technically speaking, a girl, more of a woman in her forties. Her eyes were glossy and wide with fatigue. I stepped closer and she raised the Glock at me. I could see that there was sand in the barrel, so I figured the gun had fallen on the ground. Probably when she hit the guy with the rock.

"Don't move!" The woman had an accent.

I said, "You've left the safety on, and you probably don't have a round chambered. I'm not going to hurt you. I'm going to help you."

She smiled. "Nice try. There's no safety on a Glock. Who are you?"

"Just a guy out walking."

"No shit. Just a guy out walking. Is there a trail? I haven't seen one."

"No trail. I was walking cross country and saw the buzzards."

"You have water?" I nodded. She said, "Slowly."

I unslung my backpack and pulled out a water bottle. She took it, pulled on it, hard. Didn't spill anything. She said, "You have more?" I nodded, and she lifted the plastic bottle to her mouth again.

When she was done drinking, I said, "So what happened?"

She straightened, eyes circled up and around. "I'm not yet ready to believe that you're just a guy out walking, like a tourist. It's too improbable."

"I agree, but there it is."

She shrugged. "Okay, mister tourist. Besides that one, there are others who want to kill me. They probably saw you already. If not, they heard you calling out. Maybe they're going to want to kill you as well."

I pointed toward the dead guy down the hill. "Who was that, your Coyote? Let me guess, he was a nice guy who wanted to rape you."

She nodded. "Yes and yes. He got what he deserved."

I said, "No doubt. Outstanding work. You've done a good job all around. Ought to be proud of yourself."

She frowned. "Thank you."

I said, "I'm guessing that you're part of a larger group crossing over, and now the others are looking for you, is that it?"

She said, "That's sort of the way it is, but not exactly."

A wolf whistle shrieked out from up on top of the ridge. It was followed by a responding whistle from further off. The woman looked at me with wide eyes. I nodded and spoke softly. "How many?"

"Two."

I said, "No big deal. If you give me that gun, I can help you."

"I'm not giving you the gun. I'm going to use it myself."

It might work, her with the Glock against two guys, similarly armed. Or it might not, if they had more experience, and if she had less experience. Judging by the sand in the barrel, she did not have experience with firearms.

I shrugged. "It will be harder to help you without the gun. Not impossible, but slightly more difficult. It's going to be tough for you to get them both. They won't come at the same time. Have you shot anyone before?"

The wolf whistle came again, and a voice cried out in Spanish, which I don't speak. I could see the woman's mind racing, thinking, computing, weighing things up. Using intuition and rational calculation. Figuring out if I was someone she could trust. Deciding, on the balance, maybe yes, maybe no. Then leaning on the side of a temporary and cautious maybe. On my side there was no hesitation.

She handed me the Glock. I took it, and quickly slid the action back. One in the chamber. I dropped the magazine, fine. Judging by the weight it was full, fourteen rounds. Plus one in the chamber. Fifteen total. Good to go.

I said, "Go closer to the dead guy and call them over. Tell them there's been an accident."

She hissed. "They won't believe me."

"Doesn't matter. We just need to draw them out."

I walked about fifteen feet up the ravine to a large boulder that was out of sight from the higher ground. I got down in the crease between boulder and hillside. The woman raised her head and shouted something in Spanish. A couple of rapid-fire words were shouted down in reply. I was in the shadow of the boulder, and could not see. I could only hear. Footsteps shuffled above me on the ridge top, and stones tumbled down the hill. Then, the sound of footwear sliding, an increase in pebbles rolling, and the grunted breathing of a city dweller dealing with the wilderness.

I peered around the boulder. The woman was there, crouched in the shade near the Coyote's corpse. The buzzards were not afraid, relentlessly feeding. A man came into view, and spoke more quietly, in a questioning tone. The woman responded, speaking in a matter-of-fact way. The guy was wearing a white t-shirt, baseball hat, jeans, and cowboy boots. He had his back to me, a pistol grip stuck out of the waistband of his jeans. I waited for the second guy, wanting to get them both lined up. The man in the white t-shirt spoke again, faster and harsher. She said something in response, slower and quieter than him. He grunted something back. Then, he reached behind him and took hold of his weapon. I raised the Glock and sighted on his white t-shirt. Problem was, the woman was on the other side of him.

Then I heard another man's voice, higher pitched, a little out of breath, like he'd just caught up. I moved further over to see around the boulder. The second guy was there with them. He had come up the other side, from below. The second guy was dressed the same way: t-shirt, jeans, cowboy boots, baseball hat. This guy's t-shirt was green, with a Green Bay Packers logo. He had his arms down at his sides, relaxed, like they'd found what they needed to find and were about a minute away from being done with the mission. I decided there was not going to be a better angle, or a better time. The woman was on the other side of the first guy, but crouched low and to my left. I sighted the Glock on the white t-shirt, and pulled. The Glock didn't kick hard. The polymer frame absorbing well. A bright red hole bloomed between the guy's shoulder blades. I took three steps forward, nice and easy. The gun was up and sighted. The green t-shirt guy had a momentary paralysis, as his brain cogitated what had just happened. That was all the time I needed to put a bullet into his chest.

The buzzards scooted away at the gunshots. Then, returned a few seconds later. I walked up to the white t-shirt guy and put another round into his head. I did the same for the Green Bay Packers guy. The birds repeated the same dance. The woman recoiled against the rocks.

She said, "Was that necessary?"

I said, "You told me they were going to kill you. Now they aren't going to kill you. Is that complicated?"

"Yes, I mean no, it isn't complicated. I meant about shooting them in the head."

"It was necessary."

The buzzards were all over the fresh kill. I shooed them away to retrieve weapons from both corpses. I cleared the guns and put them in my backpack. The two had matching Smith & Wesson M&P semi-automatic pistols. Like they had been equipped from the same armory. The woman stared in fascination at the bodies, crowded with vultures jockeying for the feed. At the bottom of the ravine we leaned against the rocks in the shade. We were five miles from Mule Ears road and the rental car.

I said, "Let's get out of here."

She nodded. I held out the Glock to her.

"You want this back?"

She shook her head.

The woman took more water. She was keeping her distance from me, crouched back against the ochre rocks. It was hot. The desert was wide open, but the heat was close and stifling. Both of us were covered in a film of sweat mixed with dirt. She was wearing close fitting old jeans, a gray t-shirt, and had a fleece sweater wrapped around her waist. She tossed the water bottle back and looked at me. I tipped the bottle and looked back at her over it. Maybe ten years older than me, but in good physical shape, athletic even. She was good looking. No belongings, no water, just her and the clothes she was wearing.

I said, "I'm parked about an hour and a half hike from here. Let's get to the car, and take it from there."

Her eyes were big and bright with curiosity and intelligence. She said, "Okay."

I SET THE PACE, fast. We did not speak. We walked. I stopped twice along the way and she seemed grateful for the pause and the drink, but if she was in pain, or suffering in some way, she did not say. By the time we got close to the rental car it was well into the afternoon. But we stopped well before the car, at the top of a stony ridge that looked down upon the end of Mule Ears road, which was a loop of asphalt. From up high we could clearly see my blue Ford rental maybe five hundred yards away on the valley floor. A big white Chevy Tahoe patrol vehicle was parked behind it. The Tahoe had a green stripe on the back door and flashers on the roof, border patrol.

This was border country, a constant flow of migrants passed through here every day of the week, every week of every month of every year. The border patrol was stretched thin, but they did what they could. I took a long pull on the water bottle and watched. Nothing moving. If there were cops in there, they were enjoying the AC, perhaps napping. I passed the water to the woman next to me. She drank thirstily. From that vantage point I could see the road snaking out for several miles. Mule Ears road went in a straight line along the valley floor, and then cut around and through a rocky cluster in a series of bends, like a snake track.

I pointed and said, "See over there, where the road bends around the rocks?"

She followed my gesture. "I see it."

"Get yourself to the other side of the rocks. Should take you twenty minutes. I'll wait until you're there, then I'll go down. I expect the border cops will come behind me, because there's nothing else to do where they are. But they'll wait a minute or two first."

"What if they come right after you?"

"Then I'll be back when I can, you just sit tight."

The woman nodded carefully, evaluating the situation in her own way. Wondering if twenty minutes would do it. I unslung my backpack and took out the Glock and the matching M&Ps. I weighed them up and chose the Glock, not because I liked it better, but because I had test fired it. The Smith & Wessons went under a rock. I handed the Glock to her and said, "Take this." I also gave her the remains of the water, which was not much.

She said, "See you later."

I watched the woman go down the slope on the other side. It took fifteen minutes for her to get down the mountain, and wind her way around obstacles across the desert floor to the rock cluster. By then she was a small moving object against the desert. I set off down toward the car.

Five minutes later I arrived at my rental car. The border patrol vehicle was still behind the Ford. There were two cops in the Tahoe, engine running. Both of them wore sunglasses, both of them tracked me as I approached. I nodded to them and waved. They did nothing back. I unlocked the Ford with a key fob. The border cops watched. The car was scorching hot, almost unbearable to be in, which made no difference. I got into it, fired up the engine and cranked the AC. I swung the Ford around the asphalt loop and accelerated back up Mule Ears road.

I glanced in the rearview. The Tahoe did not move. So far so good. Driving, it only took a minute to get to the cluster of rocks that had seemed distant from the ridge. Once through the sequence of turns, the rocks ended, and Mule Ears road straightened out. I stopped the car. The woman was there, running to the passenger side, opening the door, getting in, and closing it again. I drove. She snapped her seat belt in.

Ten minutes later we turned a bend and hit the intersection leading toward Texas route 118.

She said, "You got a name mister tourist?"

"Keeler."

"Looks like you saved my ass, Keeler. My name is Elena."

I LOOKED OVER AT ELENA. She was trying to stay awake, but having a hard time. The Glock rested in her lap, fingers curled loosely around the butt. Not the safest place to put a gun. The desert spread out in all directions, low rolling hills and bleached rock. The road deviated little from the straight line drawn on a map, then replicated on the ground, by men and machines, concluding at the end of Mule Ears road.

I said, "Put the gun under the seat. The drive is two hours and change. You can sleep. When we get there, we can figure out what happens next."

"The drive where?"

"I'm headed to a place called Twin Forks. You want to go someplace else?"

She said, "I need to get away from the border."

I said, "Fine. Twin Forks is away from the border."

Elena's hair was dark, with strands of gray. Her nose was not big or long, just prominent and substantial and fitting right in with the rest of her features. Cheekbones were high, eyes large. She came to a decision and nodded. The Glock went under the seat. She leaned back against the head rest and closed her eyes. She was asleep within five minutes. The road was dead straight, far as the eye could see.

I parsed the situation into its component parts.

Here was an illegal who had crossed over the Rio Grande. That much was routine. The terrain was tough in that location, which made it a good crossing point. One of the Coyotes had taken a liking to Elena, and tried to help himself, also routine. She had defended herself. Not routine. Pretty much unheard of. Which made her a special case. I figured that Elena's belongings had been back at the camp, with the other illegals. Maybe her money too. Now she had nothing except what she wore on her back.

There were no ethical questions that needed resolving. No gray areas of philosophy that I needed to weigh. A brave and resilient woman was in deep shit. A perfect candidate for assistance. There was no need to consider the medium to long term, only the short-term urgency of getting her safe. Bringing her to Mallory's place was out of the question. It was my problem, not theirs.

Elena needed to clean up, get fed, and get into some clean clothes without holes in them. Then we would see. I looked at her again. My mother had come to the US from France, and this country was all the better for it. Defending herself successfully against an armed rapist made Elena a valuable future citizen.

The Desert Inn was a low and flat, fake stucco building in pink and beige, set across Texas route 117 from the gas station where I had eaten breakfast. The sign out front announced free Wi-Fi, HBO, and a discount for members of the American Association of Retired Persons. The rooms were side-by-side, built around the parking lot in a half rectangle. I pulled the car in on the other side of the lot from the office. The only vehicle in the lot was an old Dodge, parked next to the office. Elena was awake by then and looking around.

I said, "I'm going to get a room. You wait here."

"Why are you getting a room? I need to get the hell away from here. Can't you just drop me at a bus station?"

"I can do that, but take a look at yourself. The Border Patrol will pick you up in under five minutes if I let you out."

Elena pulled the rearview mirror to her, and appraised herself. She was dusty, dirty, bloody, and scratched up. Thorns and burrs were stuck to her shirt and jeans. She pushed the mirror back. "Why are you helping me?"

"No reason except you need help."

She thought for a minute. "I appreciate the help, but nothing is going to happen in that room." She looked up at me.

I said, "Fine by me. Like I said, it's up to you. If you want me to drop you off somewhere I can."

Elena thought, then nodded her head slowly and made the call. "Okay, let's do it like you said. It makes sense. And thank you."

She dug her thumb and forefinger under the waistband of her jeans, pulled up a money belt. She said, "How much is a room here?"

I said, "When I drop you off somewhere, we can settle up. For the moment, I'll pay."

Elena looked at me for a while, and then nodded her head. "Okay."

The guy in the office was a pimply kid with a pink face wearing a red baseball hat. The kid was looking at a phone with his feet up on the counter when I came in. I asked what kind of rooms he had. He said he had a room with one large double bed for $63. I told him I would take it, and he pushed a clipboard at me with a form. I wrote my name as Earl Campbell. Campbell was a legendary running back, first pick of the NFL 1978 draft, played for the Houston Oilers, which I found appropriate.

I slid the clipboard back at the kid, and he looked down at it. "I need a copy of your ID Mister Campbell."

"It's in the car, I'll bring it by later."

The kid looked at me smugly. "Seventy-three without ID."

I counted three twenty-dollar bills, and added three singles to it. Put that down on the counter, and said, "Sixty-three dollars. Next time you open your mouth the price goes down to fifty-three."

"County Sheriff's office is just down the street, right across from the highway patrol. Want me to get those boys up here?"

"Kid, the stakes are low. I can forget the fact that you're trying to extort me, or I can not forget it. You choose, but hurry up."

He laughed quietly. "I was only messing with you."

I said nothing.

The boy pulled down a key attached to a fist sized plank of wood with the number three carved into it.

He said, "Third door down."

I looked out the window. The Ford was parked at the end, maybe the fifteenth door down.

"I'm already parked up there, can you give me the closest room to the car?"

"Take your pick buddy."

I said, "The one in front of the blue Ford over there."

He took the key back and exchanged it for room twelve. "Knock yourself out."

It was hot as hell out, and so damn dry that sweat evaporated before it could form into beads on a forehead. The landscape looked like the color had been sucked out of it, along with the moisture.

I walked back to the Ford rental.

Twin Forks was not so much a town as a settlement, clustered around a bend in Texas route 117. It was laid out in a grid extending maybe five or six blocks either side of the road. The middle two or three blocks of the grid looked like a town. Sheriff's office, General Store, barber's shop for the men, hair salon for the women, institutions of collective living. The edge of the grid where the motel sat looked more like a rocky patch of dirt with tumbleweeds and buildings spaced widely apart and nothing but scrub and sand between them.

The room was bare bones, but large enough. It fit a double bed, with plenty of space to walk around. Next to the door, a big window faced out to the parking lot, covered by heavy beige curtains. The bed was the same color, beige. On the other side of the bed was the bathroom entrance on the left side, and a wall closet on the right. A cheap drop ceiling went from the front door to where the bathroom area started. A yellow stain spread across the foam squares toward the back. Once the bathroom started, a sheet rock ceiling took over. I figured the duct work was up there. I opened the closet doors. An empty clothes rack, a shelf, and below the shelf, an ironing board leaned against the back. Above the shelf was a cavity where the sheet rock wall should have been. I looked into it and could see ducts going up to the ceiling.

There was a desk with a chair, a TV up on the wall, and ventilation grille for the AC. Elena sat on the bed and put her face in her hands. Then, a minute later, she leaned over on her side and lay her head on one of the pillows. The Glock was on the night table.

She mumbled, "I'm sorry, I can't keep my eyes open. Do you mind if I sleep?"

I said, "I'm going out for a bit. Don't leave the room, just in case."

"Okay."

A half minute later, she was making a light purring sound. I figured she might have been up two days, or more. The Coyotes like to travel at night, and during the day she would not have felt safe dropping her guard. Hard to go to sleep when rapists and cutthroats are around. When I saw that her breathing was regular, I pulled out the chair from the desk and carried it over to where the drop ceiling ended. I stood on the chair and lifted one of the ceiling tiles, slid the Glock up there, and replaced the tile. The wood plank attached to the key did not fit in my pocket, which I guess was the point. So, I took the key off the ring and left the wood in the motel room, locking the door behind me.

THE GENERAL STORE was next to the Sheriff's office, the two buildings separated by a parking lot. I pulled the Ford off the main road and into one of the slots. As soon as I pushed open the car door, dry heat hit like a wall. It felt like my hair had been blown back by an explosion. I walked across the lot, and onto the sidewalk, swung open the door to the General Store, and the weather changed once again. From the Sahara to the Arctic in one step. The AC was cranked ridiculously high. Two women were stocking items on shelves, they both wore sweaters.

One of them was taller than the other, older too.

When I asked the tall lady if they had a women's clothing section, she pointed me to the back of the store.

"Got some, not much. You want more you'll have to go to the Walmart up near Midland airport. About a half hour drive if you turn left on 117."

The sales associate said, "If you can stand the stink."

I said, "This is going to be fine ma'am, my sister isn't picky."

The older, taller one chortled at that. "Your sister, huh? Never met a woman yet who wasn't picky when it came to clothes. But, I'll take your money."

In the back of the store there was a women's section and a men's. The basics were covered. A couple of choices for each category. A carefully selected mix of home wear and work wear. I had no problem choosing the items, size was the issue. Luckily, the sales assistant looked about the same size as Elena, maybe smaller by an inch here or there. I told the women that my sister's luggage had been lost at the airport.

The tall lady laughed. "I am real sorry about your sister's luggage. But that is exactly what happens when you get all high and mighty and change the name of an airport from plain old Midland Airport, to Midland Air and *Space* Port."

The sales associate chimed in. "Like they're gonna be living on Mars next year."

Apparently, space travel was going to be the next big thing, according to the people running Midland Air and Space Port.

I picked out a pair of jeans, a t-shirt, pair of socks, and underwear. I figured Elena's fleece would be alright. The tall lady said, "What about a bra, it's a woman right?"

I shrugged, and looked lost. She took pity on me and said, "Let's make it simple. Small, medium, or large?"

"Medium I guess."

The saleswomen at the General Store had a couple of other suggestions to make, related to color and style. I agreed with everything they said, and paid with a card. The tall one waved me out the door. "You can always come on by and exchange or return if you like."

I left the store and stepped back into the heat. If anything, it had increased. Nothing moved out there except a couple of lizards skitting across the sidewalk. Certainly, no warm-blooded creatures were voluntarily outside of a climate controlled enclosure, like a car, a building, or a hole in the ground. The only people out there were moving in vehicles with tightly closed windows, and there were not many of them. Which is why I noticed the gold Jeep Cherokee parked across the main road and back a hundred yards, just outside of a place with a Law Offices, Attorney Services sign. Two guys sat alert in the front seats. Both wore baseball caps, one was shorter than the other, both were looking in my direction.

I had been a civilian now for about two years. But before that I wasn't a civilian. Before that, I had been someone who would routinely be looking out for guys sitting in cars watching for me. Except that hadn't been in Texas, but in places like Iraq, Somalia, or Northern Syria. I looked away from the Cherokee and walked back toward the Ford rental. Two questions, why, and how.

I started on how. Two ways, the border patrol officers, or Elena. Border cops could have been in the narco's pockets, waiting there at the end of Mule Ears road. In that scenario they just needed to note down the license plate number of the Ford. In the realm of possibility, not a done deal. Scenario two was simpler, Elena was carrying a phone that was being tracked.

The why of it was not difficult either. Elena was not a regular illegal. With her looks and her poise that was obvious.

I fired up the Ford and made a left out of the parking lot. Drove nice and slow and watched in the rearview as the Cherokee pulled a u-turn across 117. I got the Ford up to cruising speed. The Cherokee laid off the gas and settled back a couple hundred yards. If they had found me via the license plate, it was possible that they would not know about the Desert Inn. Maybe they had lucked out and found the Ford parked in the General Store's lot after cruising through town looking for it.

I drove past the motel and took a good look. Nothing different, in fact nothing happening at all. I pictured the inside of room twelve, Elena asleep and the Glock accumulating dust up in the ceiling. I pressed the gas pedal. Not like I was going to outrun them. The Ford was not going to outrun anything.

I thought about the moral and ethical implications of the situation, in terms of life and death. The guys in the Jeep Cherokee, a new crew. Associated to the dead guys out in the desert, but different. Back there, the situation had been a clear and present danger to life, mine and Elena's. The dead guys had been prepared to rape and kill, deadly weapons in hand. These two in the Cherokee were not there yet. I wasn't going to reset the books, not entirely, but they were not up for immediate execution either. I needed them off my back and out of action. That was all for the time being.

The Cherokee stayed on my tail for the half hour it took to get up to the Walmart.

THE WALMART WAS SET in the back of a giant parking lot. There was a gas station on the closest corner, then across the parking lot was the big box store. Next to it on the right was a cinema multiplex. On the right of that was an area for smaller stores, tucked away, owned and operated by regular people, like fish living in a shark's mouth, feeding off of the stuff left between teeth.

I wove the Ford through the rows of parked vehicles, and found a spot on the east side of the lot, close to the Walmart entrance. The women at the General Store had said something about the stink up here, and it was true. The place smelled like sulfur, which I figured was a side effect of the oilfield operations. Driving up I had seen endless fields of nodding extraction rigs.

The Walmart store was the size of a football field, and cold.

I could see a banner with Hardware written on it, maybe half a football field away. I got a basket and started shopping. Duct tape was easy. I wanted some big bearings, or something heavy like that. They had good sized padlocks, but it wasn't really what I had in mind. I spotted a baseball hat rack, and chose a red one, no logo. I pulled down a pair of thick socks, and a plain blue t-shirt from a rack of work clothing.

A man was up on a ladder scanning bar codes on boxes of screws. I asked him where the gun section was, and he pointed me in the right direction. I wanted ammo for the Glock. Given that there were a couple of guys following me. I had fired four rounds in the desert, which left eleven in the magazine. Might be enough, or it might not, depending on how things panned out.

The gun section was in Sporting Goods, which had an entire wall devoted to billiard balls. I had a eureka moment when I saw a white cue ball in a shrink-wrapped package. The cue ball went in the basket. The gun section was past a long row of bicycles. They had bikes for girls and boys, men and women, and a long tandem bike for men with women, or men with men, or two women. Any combination was feasible. At the other side of all those bikes, was a wall case filled with rows of rifles and shotguns. In front of that was another display case at counter level. Between the wall and the display case was a female Walmart associate with a puff of white hair and big framed glasses. She was talking to a wide framed guy in a red polo shirt and cargo shorts.

I was too far away to catch the conversation, but I could see from her expression that it was not going well. That is, her own position was decided, but the customer was upset. The woman shook her white puff of hair, said something. The guy she was talking to gestured, throwing his hands up in frustration. Even from that distance I could see it was the guy from the gas station grill, Caleb. Baseball hat over long hair. I had given him two dollars that morning to buy his breakfast.

The Walmart Associate was speaking calmly, hands flat on the counter. She had a face like a wall of pastry dough, with pragmatic prescription lenses. No way Caleb was going to get past that. He was blowing air, literally fuming with rage. Caleb turned around, and we made eye contact. There was not even a hint of recognition. He stormed away on thick pale legs.

When I arrived at the counter, the woman gave me an exasperated, but proud look. As if she had done a difficult, but important job. "I just couldn't sell that man a rifle. The system had him flagged, and I take my responsibilities seriously."

I said, "No doubt. You are the last line of defense. What was the flag, mental health issues?" This guy, Caleb, had been agitated that morning, he'd spoken about being on medication that prevented him from drinking coffee. He'd also spoken about shooting someone.

She nodded, "I am the last line of defense. Yes, there was a mental health flag." She was exasperated. "Why would a guy like that want to purchase a gun like that, if it weren't for no good reason?"

"What was he trying to buy?"

She gave me a *can you believe it* look, and pronounced the model and brand with exaggerated accuracy. "Sig Sauer M400 semiautomatic rifle. What they call an assault *style* rifle" She pointed behind her to a military style assault rifle with a collapsible stock. "I am going to enter his details into the denied database."

"Go right ahead, I'm in no rush."

She reached for the computer mouse. "I got him to fill out the form, so I could have all his details, you know, to enter into the computer. He thought he was getting the gun, until I told him he was denied. Then he got all upset. Not the first time I've done that. They always get real upset."

"How long is he denied for?"

"Goes out to all the licensed firearms dealers in the nation, thirty-day denial. Hopefully by then he'll have worked through his issues. If he doesn't get a gun privately. That's something we can't control. Don't need a background check for private sales." She looked up at me. "Did you see the tattoos on his face? Two tears. That means he's killed two people."

I said, "I doubt that."

She looked at me for a moment, frozen in thought, then she broke out of it. "Might take five minutes to do the form. What were you looking for?"

"Looking for 9mm ammunition."

She stood up straight. "We don't carry handgun ammunition anymore, just rifle and shotgun."

"No problem ma'am." The glass top of the display case offered a selection of knives. They had a Ka-Bar folding knife on sale that looked good. I said, "I'll take the Ka-Bar knife there."

"Folding one with the black blade?"

I said, "That's the one."

She opened the display case from the back and brought out a new knife in its own box. "It's got a clip on the handle, you can secure it in your pocket, so it doesn't fall out if you're running or something."

"Useful, in case I decided to take up jogging you mean."

"That's exactly right." She smiled, "Or wanted to take a Zumba class."

I said, "Won't happen, not in a million years."

She said, "Glad to hear it."

The Walmart had two entrances. One in the front, one on the side. I had walked in the front, now I was going to walk out the side. I paid for my items, and carried the bag to the bathroom, other side of the checkout.

Inside the stall I ripped open the packages. The t-shirt replaced my dirty white one. Baseball hat went on my head. The knife went in my pocket. The cue ball went in the sock, which went in the other sock. I held my double sock package by the neck and started twisting. When I got a good solid twist going, I pinned it down on my thigh, and got out the duct tape. I started taping with the twist. Unrolling the tape a little at a time, overlapping layers, reinforcing the twisted fabric, until the duct tape formed a good solid handle. I continued taping over the cue ball, two layers. In the end I had a serviceable impact weapon, heavy at the cue ball end, durable, with a flexible handle that could build up snap velocity and energy storage at the point of impact. Good to go.

WHEN I CAME out of the big box store, the sun had done a wonderful thing. It was low on the horizon, which made the parking lot almost beautiful, bathed in the golden rays of sunset. The shopping complex was a popular place, with hundreds of cars lined up next to each other, in dozens of rows. Here and there people were pushing carts laden with packages.

I walked straight out the side entrance and let the light foot traffic carry me up a feeder lane between parked cars. The lot continued up a slight incline, until it ran into the gas station. Beyond that were islands of yellowed grass bordered by a concrete curb. I started to work my way around from the side area to the front, keeping a look out for a gold Jeep

Cherokee. I found it a minute later, parked predictably about thirty yards back from my Ford rental. I kept another car between myself and the Cherokee, squatted down to tie my boot laces and took a good look through the other car's windows.

The Jeep Cherokee is a squat, bug like sports utility vehicle with four doors and a big hatchback trunk. I could see two guys in baseball caps, upright in the front seats, facing front. One of them was smoking a cigarette. The passenger side window was open and a tanned elbow was resting, half out of the car. I crept up behind the Cherokee on the driver's side. Stopped against the rear bumper and waited. I couldn't be crouching there forever. The issue was going to be people passing by who might observe what I was about to do, which, from an eyewitness perspective, would resemble an unprovoked violent attack on two guys minding their own business.

On the other side of the Cherokee, a woman was pushing a shopping cart, and finding it to be a challenge. The wheels were rocking over the asphalt, making a racket. A younger man moved to help her, maybe her fully grown son. On one hand there was the possibility of them witnessing what was about to go down, on the other hand the noise they were making was good cover, and maybe they would be absorbed in their own issues anyway. Maybe the trunk was complicated, maybe the bags were heavy for them.

I figured that now was as good a time as any.

I slipped the cue ball sap out of my pocket. It was comfortable to hold, and nicely weighted for the job at hand. I snuck a peak through the rear window. The driver was talking to the passenger, looking at him. Which meant he was not looking at the side mirror. I shuffled in a crouch to the door behind the driver. Took the handle, slow and careful. No sound from inside, no movement. No face looking surprised at me in the side mirror. I had the sap in my right hand, my left on the door handle. I was crouched down and ready. It would all be over in about five seconds, or it wouldn't, and that would be bad. Hopefully the shoppers were absorbed in putting their purchases away. Whatever.

I pulled the door and launched into the back seat of the Cherokee in a single movement. My legs catapulted me into the car and up on the seat. I held onto the driver's head rest with my left hand for leverage. The driver had a millisecond to turn toward me in surprise, before the sap crashed into his temple and his head flopped left, toward the car door. I whipped the weapon across at the passenger. Caught a glimpse of him grimacing and turning toward me. The passenger had more time to react, and his hand came up, defending against the blow. The defense worked, to some degree. He partially blocked my arm, but the cue ball end snapped around on the flexible handle, smacking into his mouth. The point of impact was upper lip, a tooth caved in, blood from the lip spurted. His eyes bulged and he stiffened in shock. I pushed his defending hand down with my free hand, and sent another back handed sap shot at him. The duct taped cue ball thudded into the side of his head, and he flopped over, like the other guy.

They would be out cold for a minute or two.

I looked out the windshield. Nothing happening, nobody alerted. The shoppers were packing the back of a Toyota. All good. The driver's head was forward, against the steering wheel. The other guy's torso was slumped into the foot well.

He had blood on his face. I dove over the front seat and fished in his jeans. Came up with a wallet and a Colt .45. It was the 1911 model, nice gun. America's favorite. The other guy had a wallet and a Ruger LCP in .38 caliber. Ugly gun. I fished in the wallets. The driver's ID had been issued in the state of Texas, name was Alvarez. The other guy was Vasquez-Garcia, with a driver's license out of New Mexico. Between them they were carrying almost a thousand dollars in cash.

I took the money, the ID cards, and the guns. Tossed the emptied wallets into the driver's side footwell. I slipped out of the car. The Ka-Bar knife I had bought was factory sharp. I stayed on the inside of the parked car, between the Cherokee and its closest neighbor. The blade slipped easily into the side wall of the Jeep's tire, compressed air rushed out in an angry hiss. I slit the two tires on the driver's side. When I was done, the driver was coming to. I opened the door and the guy looked at me, cross eyed. I put a solid left hook into his jawline, he slipped back into the fog.

On the way back to the motel I stopped the Ford next to a storm drain, opened the door and dropped both pistols into it. I didn't know what those two guys had been up to with their weapons. Did not want to find out either.

NAVIGATING the town was like running a finger along the lines of a checkerboard. I turned off route 117, a couple of grid lines north of the Desert Inn. Left two blocks, right three blocks, right again one block. Which brought me around the back of the motel, a plain building planted like its neighbors, in a wide rocky lot. The sun was still in the process of disappearing, and the barren desert settlement looked almost romantic in the glow. Flat roofed homes were set in generous but dusty lots, sprinkled with big cactus plants, the occasional evergreen tree, rusting automobile shells and engine parts. A boat was improbably hoisted onto blocks in the yard across the street. There weren't any people outside.

I PARKED the Ford with two wheels up on a dusty curb. Picked up the bag with new clothes from the passenger seat. Next to the bag was my homemade cue ball sap. One side of the silver duct taped ball had a red stain. I put it in the glove compartment. As an afterthought, I threw the red baseball hat in there with the sap.

The back of the Desert Inn was unpainted cinder block wall, lined with a gravel filled drainage ditch. The roof featured a row of air conditioning units, one for each room. I came around the side and leaned casually against the edge of the half rectangle of motel rooms. It was a decent observation post, screened by a spiky desert plant the size of a small tree. A red pickup truck had parked close to the motel office. It had not been there before, which on its own was not suspicious. The old Dodge was still there, poking out on the other side of the pickup truck. The Dodge probably belonged to the kid in the office. Other than that, there was nothing going on. Opposite the motel, route 117 made a horizontal line. Beyond that, the gas station seemed far away. Once in a while a vehicle passed on the road. Other than that, no parked cars, no watchers in trees.

I rolled off the building, stepped around the cactus, and onto the footpath protected by a long awning. Got to room twelve and knocked twice. No answer. I opened the door with the key and looked inside. The bed was empty, sheets ruffled. I closed the door, and stepped in. Elena spoke from behind me. "You took a long time."

I turned around. She was standing in the corner with the Glock in her hand.

I threw the Walmart bag on the bed. Pulled the driver's license cards I had taken from the two in the Cherokee out of my pocket and showed them to Elena. "Know these guys?"

She said, "And you took the key." Then, she grabbed the identity cards out of my hand and sat on the bed.

"What are those?"

"Couple of guys who were following me."

Elena swept a lock of hair from her forehead. She studied the license cards, looked up at me. "How did you get their driver licenses?"

"I took them, without asking, or saying please, if that's what you mean." She grinned; it was like the sun coming out. I said, "Do you recognize them?"

"No, but that doesn't mean anything."

"What doesn't mean anything?"

"That I don't know who they are." She drew one long leg under her, put the gun on the night table. "Look, you don't understand, and you don't need to get involved. This is my problem."

I said, "They were following me, which makes it my problem now."

"Tough guy, huh?"

I said nothing.

She laughed sharply and said my name, "Keeler," which, in her accent sounded the same as if she was saying Killer. Elena handed the license cards back to me. "I'm afraid there will always be men identical to these *cabrons*. The sicarios will not stop coming until I am dead. They were following you?"

"Yes."

"So, then we were seen in your car."

"Looks that way."

"That Border Patrol vehicle maybe."

I said, "Or your phone."

She touched the bulge in her front pocket. "You think?"

I said nothing.

Elena rubbed her eyes and sighed. "Keeler, I've been running for a long time. Crossing over wasn't even Plan B, it was more like Plan D. What do you do when Plan D fails?"

I said, "Revise the plan."

"Easy for you to say." She looked at the plastic bag on the bed.

"Hope they fit, probably won't."

She said, "That was nice of you."

"What do they have against you?"

Elena picked up the plastic bag and set it to the side. She said, "I'm a reporter. I decided to write about what everyone knew, but was afraid to say. All of those mayors and cops and officials and important assholes, all lying and caught up in the narco-state. I just started to write about it simply, with no thought other than to tell the truth. It felt great, Keeler. Really great." Elena shifted forward on the edge of the bed, hung her feet down. She looked at me with wide eyes. "It was the stupidest thing I could have imagined doing. I have no idea what got into me. I was surprised that at first, nothing happened. I wrote articles. They got published in the paper. People read them. People commented online, positive and supportive comments. As if everything was normal, you know what I mean?" I nodded. "Nothing happened for two months, and then, they cut the throats of my editor, and his entire family, and strung their bodies from the overpass outside of town, with perverted jokes written on cardboard signs hung around their necks. The next day I got a postcard in the mail; it said, 'We are going to rape you until you die.'"

I said, "Have a shower, get changed. We should get something to eat. Then we can talk about plan D."

Elena said, "Optimism. I like it."

She slid out of the bed and went around the side, picked up the plastic bag with the clothes, and went into the bathroom. I lay down on the bed and looked at the ceiling. I could help Elena get away from the border area, that wouldn't be a problem. But, what would she do then? It's not easy living as an illegal, especially if she had been a journalist. It's one thing hooking into the network of illegals working the jobs that run the American economy. Construction, lawn work, restaurants, care work, house cleaning. But that is not the same as getting a real job on the books. And, there is always the danger of a knock on the door from ICE. Then deportation back to Mexico, and the sicarios. I thought about Canada, maybe she could claim asylum, if she could make a plausible case that her life was in danger. I had read that Canada had a visa free entry to Mexicans, at least they used to. If we could get Elena over the border, she could make a claim there. The sound of the shower started up in the bathroom.

But moving to Canada would not solve the problem of the sicarios finding her, if they were determined. Not easy to see what would help.

I walked to the big window and drew the curtain back. The last glowing edge from the top of the sun was kissing the horizon. From the big window I could make out the back of the red pickup truck parked near the office, beyond it, the front grille of the old Dodge. Otherwise, the lot was empty. A light flashed on the other side of route 117, the flash of two headlights. My eyes snapped to the spot, and I made out the shadow of a pickup truck. It had not been there before. A darkened shape silhouette against the lights of the gas station, parked facing the motel, other side of the main road. The high beams flashed again, once.

Flashing high beams is a way of signaling. In the best case scenario, it was an innocent thing. Maybe a couple of lovers were in the truck, they had accidentally triggered the high beams. Or maybe some kid was learning morse code and flashing signals to his friend a mile away. Or maybe the sicarios really were that determined. Maybe the guys in the

Jeep Cherokee had identified the Ford at the Desert Inn, before I left to go shopping. Then had followed me all the way to Walmart. In that case, taking them out had not been smart, because it had prompted them to call in reinforcements. Now, instead of one bunch of guys, we could be facing two or three.

HOPE FOR THE BEST, plan for the worst. The worst was bad, the second team coming in as back up. Four guys minimum, approaching with weapons. Fanning out to cover exit options. We had to get out of the room, but the front door was not an attractive option.

It was a real humdinger.

I KNOCKED on the bathroom door. The shower was going. No answer. I knocked again, the shower stopped. I opened the door a crack and spoke into it. "Get out of the shower and get dressed, we have to leave."

Elena said, "How long?"

"Maybe two minutes, maybe less."

"Okay."

I closed the door. Retrieved the Glock from the night table, put it in my waist band at the back. I jammed the desk chair under the door knob, two of the legs were up in the air, the carpet helped with the grip. I reconsidered. They had seen me pull the curtain open. But that was from a distance, with a spotting scope, maybe. But it was more likely that they had no scope, that they had just seen movement and interpreted it. If that was the case, they would have doubts. If there was a chair jammed under the door knob, there would be zero doubt.

Operators deal in enemy doubt. Doubt could save us a minute or two.

I removed the chair and put it back under the desk. I put my head into the closet. The upper part of the wall was just a cavity. I pulled my head out, to check on Elena. She was coming out of the bathroom with wet hair, adjusting her money belt to fit under the new jeans.

I said, "Good to go?"

She was looking around. All action, minimal reflection. Like a pro, which made sense, with her experience. "Good, yes. Where's the gun?"

I patted the small of my back. "I've got it, you want it?" Elena shrugged. She was holding her phone. I pointed to it. "Leave that here."

"Why?"

"Might be how they found us. Those things are tracking devices. Just leave it here."

She placed the phone on the desk, next to the TV. I said, "We're going up into the ceiling," and pointed at the closet.

She said, "In there?"

Elena wasn't sarcastic. She was curious.

I said, "There's a way in. Might work."

"And if it doesn't?"

"If it doesn't, the gun has eleven rounds in it. I'll try and use them wisely. Plus, I've got a knife. Maybe I could use both at the same time. We'll see."

I went into the closet again. The hole was big enough to fit a person. I had no idea what we would find in there, but Elena was going first, so it would be up to her. I beckoned her over, pointed into the hole. She nodded. I cupped both hands for a boost, and she leaned one hand on my shoulder, the other braced against the closet wall. Her foot went into my cupped hands and I lifted her up.

There was a knock at the door. Elena slipped down, out of my clenched hands.

"Mierda."

I said, "Go easy." Another knock. "Ignore that."

She laughed, "Sure."

I boosted her again. This time she got her upper body fully into the hole. I was holding her left foot, she was struggling with something up there. She said, "Push me." I pushed her foot, but she was still struggling. "Push my ass." I gave her a push with both hands, and whatever it was that she was doing worked. She got a leg up and disappeared into the hole.

The lock was wiggling in the front door. I looked at it, and momentarily contemplated putting a couple of rounds through the cheap wood. Like a tight vertical triple pattern, customized for various head heights. The rounds would go through that like daggers through cotton candy. I might get one, or two of those guys. It was an attractive proposition. But I had no way to know how many of them were out there, and I had Elena to think about. There was no chance I was going to let these people get her. Getting shot would be like handing them a gift, all wrapped up in Christmas paper with a satin bow.

The door shuddered and cracked. A booted foot had gone into the area around the bolt, splintering wood. I looked up at the closet cavity. Elena was gone. I gripped the edges of the hole, boosted myself up, hoping the sheet rock would hold. So far, so good. I got a leg over, straddling the opening. It was reinforced with pine studs, thankfully not old, and not rotten. Took my weight. I stretched my free leg out to catch the closet door. The front door pounded again from another booted blow. I got the Glock out from my waistband. Worked the slider and chambered a round. I was in a compromised position. The gun was in my right hand, pointed to the door. Left hand gripping the edge of a wall stud. The wood splintered on the front door, a boot came through it, and got stuck. I heard a furious curse from the other side. Looked like the guy had fallen down with his foot in the door. I reached out again with my toe and caught the edge of the closet door. Like a ballerina or something. It wasn't a great angle, and I was in danger of opening it wider, which was the opposite of what I wanted. I allowed my toe to go up against the edge of the door, caught it, and gently eased it toward me. The closet door closed, just as another blow caved in the front door.

It was pitch black. I put the Glock in my waistband, "Elena."

She whispered, "Yes."

I could hear her shuffling, but could not see what she was doing. She was up higher than me. With the closet door closed, the space was dark. I could hear cautious movement on the other side of the door. They were inside and looking around. My body was lodged between the bathroom wall and the back of the closet, about five feet off the ground. Above me was the ceiling cavity. After being in there a few seconds, my eyes adjusted. Electrical switches built into the ceiling space and near the floor below emitted dim light. I prepared to boost up and join Elena, wherever she was. But then I noticed the outlines of a sheetrock panel leaned against the inside of the wall, just below me. It occurred to me that this was the missing panel from the back of the closet. No doubt, it had fallen into the wall during construction, and the workers had just left it there.

From the other side of the closet door came a low murmur of voices speaking in Spanish. I don't speak Spanish, but I did know that it was a matter of seconds before one of those guys opened the closet door and saw the cavity, and maybe me. It would be like shooting fish in a barrel. I took the gamble. Eased myself down into the cavity between walls, until my boots came to rest on a wooden stud, about two feet off the ground. I had maybe an inch of room between my nose and the wall. I dropped my shoulder, as far as possible and tried to reach the sheetrock piece. Managed to get thumb and forefinger on a corner, and lifted. At that point, the top of my head was level with the opening to the closet, which was dark. I got the panel up, and in front of my face, as the closet door opened. I pushed the sheetrock against the framing studs, and held it there, hoping that the guy had not seen movement. Light bloomed around the edges of the panel.

It was hot already. All of that monkeying around made it even hotter. I was sweating. My hands were slippery. I pushed hard against the sheet rock and tried to relax my arms and shoulders at the same time. I had no way of knowing if the guy on the other side was still looking around the closet. Why would he be, if there was nothing special to see.

Elena said, "Keeler."

I said nothing.

I held the sheetrock against the studs and counted off a minute in my head. How long can a guy look around an empty closet, ten seconds? I slid the panel up and looked through the gap. The closet door was half open. There was no face looking up at me, which was a good thing. But there was a guy lying on the bed looking at Elena's phone. A voice came from behind me, in the bathroom. The intervening wall muffled the sound. I couldn't understand the language anyway. Elena's shower had made the bathroom wet, plus her old clothes were on the floor, so they would be puzzling it out, the mysterious disappearance. The guy on the bed had a thick body and a shaved head with a thin mustache and beard narrowed to a point. He was wearing a white t-shirt, and had his head back on the pillow, looking up at his phone. I could see that he had a neck tattoo, but was at the wrong angle to make out the design.

I needed to put the panel down and get up into the ceiling. The question was, would the guy on the bed notice the panel moving out of the corner of his eye, or was he captivated by the screen. He answered my question, by swinging his legs over on the other side of the bed, and putting his back to me. I dropped the sheetrock carefully and let it rest against the floor. Then, I pulled myself into the upper area of the cavity. I kept on going, finding studs to place my feet.

A minute later I came against Elena. She was horizontal, laid out across ceiling joists. Between the drop ceiling and the back of the building, ducts sloped down from the air conditioners installed on the roof to ventilation grilles built into the ceiling. The sheetrock wouldn't hold us by itself, but the wood joists would. I came alongside her, brushing up against her hair. She shuffled over slightly. It was even hotter up here. I could only see her dimly, but I could feel her proximity. She smelled like soap, and I felt her breath against my neck.

She said, "I think it goes all the way across. Look."

I looked up. The crawl space above the rooms extended toward the office. I thought of the red pickup truck. It was parked close to the office, which might or might not mean that the driver of that truck was staying in an adjacent room. I figured we could crawl over and come down into a closet at least two rooms over from ours, but no more. Ours was number twelve, so maybe number nine or ten would be good.

Elena wiggled against me, and I felt her hip touching mine. Her hair got in my face and I had to blow it away. She said, "Sorry, I'm getting pins and needles."

WE CRAWLED ACROSS, one at a time, me going first, using the joists and maneuvering around the air conditioning ducts. Which were useful because they clearly marked each room. It wasn't easy to move in the crawl space and we had to be silent. Plus it was incredibly hot. So, we took our time. Two air conditioners and five minutes later, I hung down from a joist and found purchase for my toes on a horizontal wall stud. I eased myself down, far enough to make out the space between bathroom and closet wall. I got myself into the right position, unclipped the folding knife from my back pocket. I listened for a half minute, no sound coming from the other side. Which did not mean all that much, but what else did I have to go on? I put the point of the blade against the sheetrock, and used my right hand as a hammer to stab it through.

The blade went in easily. The sound was loud in the confined space. Like punching through a sheet of paper laid over a sand pit. I took the grip and pulled down, making a nice first cut. I worked down, along the stud, until I figured the hole was big enough. Then, I cut across to the next stud and completed the rectangle. I put the blade back into the original cut, and jimmied it toward me. With the sheet rock in hand, I pulled it in. The panel came off and I was looking at the inside of the closet. I slipped the sheet rock down into the wall. Climbed through the wooden framing, and slid carefully into the closet. I cracked open the door, and was looking at an empty room, the mirror image of room twelve.

I whispered into the dark, "Okay."

Elena came down, feet first. She eased herself out of the hole, the muscles on her arms were smooth and lean, and slick with sweat, doing what they needed to do. We were both soaked and dirty from crawling around in the ceiling.

I said, "Hope the shower felt good anyway. Didn't last long."

She said, "It did feel good. Feels better to be down here."

It was a lot cooler in the room than up in the ceiling. The window in room ten was the same as in room twelve, big and covered by a drawn curtain. I did not want to go near it, in case of any shadow that might be visible from outside. At least the door was intact. The problem was the same as before, only one way out. There was a phone on the desk, an old fashioned one with push buttons on a box with a handset connected by a curly wire. I picked up the handset in one hand, while punching the numbers with the other. The line gurgled a couple of times and then I got ring tone. Mallory answered.

"Yeah?"

"It's Keeler. How far out are you?"

"About a half hour. You got lonely?"

"Got a humdinger."

She said, "A humdinger?"

I said, "Yeah. A real humdinger."

"Why am I not surprised. What do you need?"

"You know the Desert Inn motel?"

"Yes."

"I'm here, stuck in a room and I need to bug out. What are you in, the Bronco I saw?"

"Yeah we're in Dad's Bronco. You're calling for a dust off."

I said, "Affirmative."

"Make that twenty-five minutes. What do I need to know?"

"Two to four MAMs outside room twelve, but I can't see. Need you to take a look and let me know. We're in room ten."

Mallory said, "Scout the front first."

"That's right. Just a drive by."

"Roger that. And then?"

I said, "I'm calling you back in twenty-five minutes. Don't call this number."

She said, "No problem."

I hung up the phone.

Elena was looking at me. "What the hell was that?"

"Friends. They'll help us out. It's going to take twenty-five minutes for them to get here."

"So what do we do now?"

I sat on the edge of the double bed, and removed the Glock from my waistband. The gun went on the night table.

I said, "Now we sleep."

"Sleep?"

"Yes, that's what we do, we sleep."

"How will you know when it's been twenty-five minutes?"

"I'll know."

I stretched out on the bed and folded my hands behind my head. Elena went into the bathroom, and I heard water running. I figured she was washing her hands. I looked at mine, filthy. I wiped them on my jeans. It did not help. Then, Elena lay down next to me. I closed my eyes and relaxed. There were no sounds from outside, except for the occasional whoosh of passing traffic on route 117. Maybe those military aged males out there were back in their vehicles with the AC on, waiting. Maybe they were pacing up and down outside room twelve. I had no way of knowing. I could feel Elena's tension. She was shifting her body around on the bed, fixing the pillow. Her breathing was tense and shallow. After a couple of minutes it got regular and deep. After that, mine did too.

I opened my eyes twenty-five minutes later.

Dave answered the phone this time. "Dave here."

I said, "Dave, what's the situation?"

"Mal's driving. We just cruised by a couple minutes ago. Currently parked up in town waiting on your call. Desert Inn lot has a red pickup and a Dodge parked near the office. Plus your rental in front of twelve."

"Nothing else going on?"

"Nada."

"I need you to take the plates off your vehicle. Then come in through the motel parking lot real slow and screen us so we can leave unobserved around the side."

"Us."

"Right. Us. Can you do that?"

"Will do. Call me back in five."

I said, "Dave."

"Yeah."

"Put me on speaker."

There was a click and a beep and then the sound changed. Dave said, "You're on speaker."

"Mallory."

Mallory said, "I hear you."

I said, "The motel is being observed from over by the gas station, across route 117. You can look for them on your way in, and confirm it when we do the thing. It's a pickup truck with roof lights."

"We'll take a look. What's the thing?"

"The thing is, you come in to the lot, drop your dad off at the office. Dave goes in to the office and asks a question. You make it up Dave."

Dave's disembodied voice said, "Okay."

"Mallory. While Dave's in the office, you're going to turn the vehicle around by driving the length of the motel and circling around at the end. Then you leave. No pausing, no stopping. We'll be using the vehicle as a screen to get out around the back. Do you follow?"

Mallory said, "Roger that. See you in five minutes."

We hung up. Elena was alert, watching me from the bed.

I said, "Five minutes."

I went to the front door, keeping close to the wall and back from the window. The door had a manual lever for the lock. I turned it and checked, it worked.

Five minutes later, Dave picked up the phone again. "Stay on the line, coming through in thirty seconds. Room ten, right?"

"That's right." I signaled to Elena to get up. Spoke into the phone, "I'm going offline. See you soon." I hung up.

The room was empty and dark, except for Elena standing by the bed and looking at me expectantly. I nodded to her, "We're going to get out of here. Stay behind me and put a hand on my shoulder. Keep your hand there. We're going to go fast, but we're not going to run. Do you understand?"

She nodded. "I think so."

I said, "My friends will come and we're going to hide behind their car, until we get to the end of the motel. Then we go around the wall to the other side."

"Sure. I'll follow you."

I went to the door, gun in hand. The Bronco rumbled outside, sounded like the eight-cylinder version, and you can hear those from half a mile away. The engine rumble came closer and then paused, as Mallory dropped her dad off at the motel office. The V8 started up again. I figured ten seconds. I counted it off and got to five, depressed the lever on the door lock. I turned round to Elena and nodded at her. She put her hand on my left shoulder. I said, "Keep the contact."

"Yes." Her breathe in my ear.

The rumbling approached. I waited until it was right on top of us, and opened the door. We stepped out quickly, as the big 4x4 nosed in. Elena closed the door with her left hand, and then we were alongside the silver Bronco, right underneath the driver's window. I held the Glock down by my thigh. We were crouched and moving with the car.

Mallory said, "We're being watched from the other side. Like you said. You got your car around the corner?"

"Out back. Meet us somewhere safe, and not your house. How about the Walmart up toward Midland, a restaurant in that complex?"

"There's a Texas Roadhouse up there."

"Fine."

We were coming up on room twelve. I put the Glock up and looked into the room as we passed. The door was closed, as much as a smashed door can be closed. Looked like the sicarios had gone away, for the time being. Elena's hand was resting on my shoulder. She was keeping up and doing great. We came around to the angle, stayed close to the Bronco as it turned. Then, we broke off and slipped through the space between the cactus tree and the wall, Elena right there with me. The Bronco growled off into the night, and we were around the corner in the dark. Safe, for the time being.

I GOT Elena behind the motel and stood at the corner, screened by the decorative tree sized cactus. I looked across route 117 at the pickup truck. It had not moved, and for a moment I thought I might have been wrong about it. But then I saw a silhouette shifting in the cab. I turned around and looked out the back. No cars with silhouettes in the front, no group of two or three guys clustered around a tree. Not even a dog slinking between the rusted car bodies and engine axles.

We walked around the side of the motel to the rear, where I had left the rental, crossed over the rock strewn area before the street. In the car, I tucked the Glock locked and cocked, between my right thigh and the seat. We drove out of town through the back roads and did not see another vehicle until we hit route 117 about a mile north of the Desert Inn. Then, the road wound gently among the foothills. Elena was suddenly curious about me. It was like a game of twenty questions.

She said, "You are from here Keeler, from Texas?"

I felt her looking at me. I looked at the road. "I don't live anywhere."

"What do you mean, you don't live anywhere?"

"Think about it as a two-phased approach to life, like time and place. I am alive, but not currently rooted to any one spot.

She said, "I have no idea what that means."

I said, "Concretely, I got my discharge from the military a couple years ago. Since then, you could say I've been traveling."

"Like a two-year vacation."

"Something like that."

She said, "Going where the wind blows."

I said, "That implies I'm a pushover, as if I don't decide and the wind does. I don't think of it that way, but it may be right.

"You are in charge, but shit happens."

"Maybe everyone thinks they're in charge of their lives, but then shit happens."

She said, "One thing is for sure, shit happens."

I said, "Damn straight it does."

"So, you are like some version of a bum."

"I have nothing against bums."

"Too handsome to be a bum. Doesn't talk like a bum. Doesn't act like a bum."

I said, "I'll take that as a compliment. Never said I was a bum, just said that I have nothing against bums and hobos."

She said, "Tough to have a relationship with a woman if you're a bum."

"I have great relationships with women."

"What about your friend, the bald girl with the scar."

I said, "I got to Texas last night. I'm here to see her."

She said, "Is your friend ok?"

"No, she's definitely not ok. She's got a brain tumor, which is why I came. To say goodbye to her."

Elena looked at me. "Goodbye, like she is going to die?"

"Correct. She's going to die. Like all of us, but in her case the appointment has been moved up in the calendar."

"Jesus. When?"

I said, "This week, tomorrow, next week, next month. Not much longer than that."

She said, "That's really awful. I'm sorry to hear it."

"That's life. Anyway, you've got your own problems."

"Everyone always prioritizes their own problems. I'm not trying to be like everyone else."

I said, "Some problems are more clear-and-present than others. Most problems don't come with armed assassins."

"That's true. Where do you know her from, your friend?"

"The Air Force. She's a combat rescue helicopter pilot."

"No shit. And you worked with her?"

I said, "I did."

Elena looked out the window. The Ford was cruising along dutifully, neither under or over powered, an uninteresting vehicle to drive. I looked at her. Her hair was blowing in the wind coming from the open window. She looked good, and I felt good. Healthy and happy.

She said, "I've never been in this country before, you believe that? I've been to Europe, South America, never been to the USA."

"You've seen the inside of a motel room, up close and personal, and the inside of a car. And the outside, looking out the window. What do you think, so far?"

"I kind of like it."

"It's a great country. Bigger than you can imagine."

"Where were you, before you came to see your friend in Texas?"

I said, "I was up in Vancouver, which is technically Canada."

"What was that like?"

"Green and blue, smelled like seaweed."

"I heard it rains a lot up there in the Pacific Northwest?"

"It does in the winter. But right now it's beautiful. Clear blue skies, not too hot, not too cold. Pretty much perfect."

She said, "But, then you had to come down to Texas for your friend. What's her name?"

"Mallory, and her dad's Dave."

"You're a good friend then. A loyal person."

"We served together. It changes things."

Elena put her hands up in her hair and manipulated it into a bun with some deft maneuvering.

I said, "What about you, where are you from?"

She said, "I'm from a place called Puerto Vallarta. Heard of it?"

"Nope."

"It's a resort town, on the Pacific coast in Jalisco."

"Like beaches and stuff."

"Beaches, restaurants, hotels. My parents ran a hotel, is how we got there. Originally from Mexico City."

I said, "Is that where you became a reporter. Did you study for that, in college?"

Elena nodded, "Lived ten years in Mexico City after college."

"Then back home to Puerto Vallarta."

"You got it."

"Why'd you go back?"

She said, "You know how it is, there was a man involved."

I said, "Is there still a man involved?"

Elena was studying the dashboard panel, worrying the surface with her fingertips. "No. There's no man involved anymore."

A half hour later we arrived at the Walmart complex. I drove in through the gas station, and crawled the car slowly into the lot for the second time that day. The parking lot sloped gently down to the buildings. Crammed with cars. Walmart on the left, Multiplex Cinemas on the right. Then, a line of smaller stores. The Multiplex building was as big as Walmart, and taller. Most of it was a plain prefab exterior with a Cinergy Cinemas sign the size of a truck slapped on it, lit up in green and white.

The Jeep Cherokee had not moved. The two slashed tires were flat as pancakes, and the guys who'd been in it were gone. Over to the right, I could see a glowing neon sign that read Texas Roadhouse.

I parked the Ford about fifty yards from the restaurant, and got out. Shoved the Glock into my waistband. Elena closed her door and I locked the car with the key fob. The Texas Roadhouse was a chain restaurant, all dressed up like it did home cooking. Which did not look likely, given the size of it. If anything was home cooked in there, it stretched the idea of 'home' pretty far. Not that I was bothered, I wasn't. I was hungry. The restaurant interior was bright, noisy, and crowded. We walked past tables covered with plastic baskets holding paper-wrapped burgers, ribs, and a variety of fried foods. I saw Elena looking, just as interested in eating as I was.

Mallory and Dave were already there, tucked into a corner booth at the back. Dave saw me first and waved us over. I slid in on the wall side, next to Dave. Elena sat alongside Mallory.

I said, "Elena, meet Dave and Mallory."

Elena said, "Pleased to meet you." Mallory and Dave reciprocated.

A busboy approached, balancing a tray, from which he unloaded a pitcher of ice water and four big glasses. When he was gone, Mallory and her dad turned to me, as if I could explain everything.

I said, "Let's order first. We skipped lunch."

Elena said, "Just lunch?"

The others got busy picking up their menus and scrutinizing them. I left mine on the table, figured the experts would know best. A uniformed waitress sidled up to our booth, an electronic tablet cradled in the crook of an elbow. She had a name tag shaped like the state of Texas, her name was Camila.

She said "Howdy folks. Got any questions, or are y'all ready to order?"

I said, "I'm hungry. You choose."

Camila did not miss a beat. She'd rehearsed her lines. "Well now, the T-bone steak is the biggest and the best, and it comes with three sides including waffle fries, coleslaw, and collard greens."

"All right then, I'll have exactly that."

"Rare, medium, or well done?"

"Rare."

Elena ordered the fillet steak, a leaner cut. Mallory and her dad both went the burger route, with plenty of extras. Waffle fries for Mallory, steak fries for Dave. We all ordered bottles of coke. Then, just in case, Dave ordered an extra side of Jalapeño poppers for the table. The waitress took our order, and used a little stylus to translate the words into taps on her tablet. When she walked away, the others looked at me.

I SAID, "After you left for the medical tests, I went out to Big Bend for a hike. Because you were gone, and I'd been cramped up in airplanes and automobiles all night and day. Five miles in, I ran across Elena." I gestured toward Elena. "Make a long story short, she was having some issues with the Coyotes running her across the border. By that, I mean she had to fight off a rapist. Hit the guy over the head with a rock. I showed up just after that."

Mallory said, "Coyote tried to rape you, and you fought him off?" Elena nodded.

Dave said, "Hit him with a rock, he get knocked out or what?" He looked at Elena.

Elena said, "The guy was lying there. Then Keeler showed up out of nowhere."

I said, "She killed him, guy was dead as a door nail. Multiple blows with a heavy object. Skull fracture, herniated brain, and a good deal of hemorrhaging. Elena took the guy out."

Elena looked at me, horrified.

Mallory said, "Nice work if you can get it, taking out rapists."

I said, "Problem is, he wasn't alone. A couple of his buddies showed up and I had to get her out of there. Why I took her out in my rental car and brought her up here to get safe."

Dave said, "You know they prosecute for bringing illegals over, these days."

"I know that. Which is why I did not want you and Mallory involved. I brought Elena to the Desert Inn and got a room. The plan was to pause and assess the situation."

"And they found you at the motel."

I said, "They found me in town first, I was coming out of the General Store, noticed I was being followed, and brought them out here to Walmart. Figure they got the plates on my rental car."

Mallory said, "Brought them to Walmart, for what, take them shopping?"

"I couldn't think of any other place to bring them. I neutralized two guys in the vehicle. Then I went back to the motel and you know the rest. Others showed up."

Dave said, "Neutralized?"

"I cracked their heads a little and slashed the tires of their vehicle." I gestured to the parking lot. "It's still out there if you're interested in seeing a Jeep Cherokee with two flat tires."

Mallory smiled and crunched on an ice cube.

Dave said, "I get that, but why would they follow you all in the first place, if they were just a bunch of Coyotes? Those traffickers are small time. It'd be highly unusual if they were to bring their business up here."

I said, "That's the question. But first off, just to finish up, Elena's not a regular illegal, she's a journalist. She says cartel people put a hit on her."

Dave and Mallory looked at Elena, sizing her up. Elena glanced back at them, and then at me, but something caught her eye and she looked up. Camila the waitress leaned over our booth and put down a big plate of deep-fried jalapeños stuffed with cheese. "There you go. Jalapeño poppers. The rest is on its way."

Elena held up a hand, "One second. I haven't eaten in a few days. I'll eat two of these first and then I have something to say." Elena carefully ate two of the jalapeño poppers, one at a time, slowly but not delicately. We watched her eating. She wiped her fingers on a paper napkin and folded it, setting the napkin down beside her plate. "I hired one Coyote." She looked at me. "That's the guy you saw with his brain leaking out of his skull. He was going to rape me. I led him on, so I could get away. The other people who were after us, down there in the desert, were sicarios with the Jalisco cartel, or they could be Sinaloa contracted out by Jalisco. Doesn't matter, right?" She took another jalapeño pepper and ate it, then continued. "I left home a couple of months ago. It took me time to set up the crossing."

Mallory raised her hand. "Question, just to give us a little background. Keeler said that you're a journalist. I'm assuming you pissed off the narcos by doing your job, is that it?"

"Like I told Keeler, I started writing stories about the links between narco trafficking and the police and administration in my hometown, Puerto Vallarta. That would have been one thing, but I think I've managed to go one step further, in that I've pissed off the boss, who calls himself El Lagarto. So, it's become a personal thing for him."

I said, "What does El Lagarto mean?"

Mallory said, "The Lizard."

Dave shook his head, "Jesus Christ."

Elena said, "I went over with the Coyote I had been recommended from a reliable source, thinking there was a sixty percent chance it would work. I didn't expect that he would lead me right into a trap with those hit men. But he did. When we got over the river, we walked up a path, over a ridge, and there were these two guys with like, sick little grins on their faces. The Coyote was even smiling. They were going to kill me right then and there, except I think that the Coyote had negotiated with them beforehand, that he'd be the first to rape me. First dibs. When I saw those sicarios, I was so scared. But somehow I had the presence of mind to play the Coyote off of them. I got him to take me away from them. Said that I would cooperate and make it good for him, like a girlfriend experience."

Mallory said, "Gross."

"The sicarios didn't like that, but the Coyote didn't care. So, I was lucky, but none of it would have worked without you." She looked over at me.

I said, "Well that's just dumb luck then. Sometimes it works that way, is that not right Mallory?"

Mallory said, "That's right." She turned to look at Elena, "You got un-fucked. That's a hell of a story, and you're one hell of a lady. I'm happy to know you."

Dave said, "So am I."

Elena put her head down. I was right across from her, and saw a tear forming at the edge of her eye. She wiped it away and lifted her head back up with a smile. "I'm just so damn hungry right now." She took another deep-fried jalapeño. "But I can't only eat these things." She smiled.

I said, "Eat them all if you want, but not too fast."

Dave looked around. "God damn it where's our food?"

I said, "Relax, it's on the way.

There was a little silence, and then Elena involuntarily laughed, and the laugh was contagious. Mallory burst into laughter, and when she was finished said, "Holy shit, I don't know if I should laugh or cry."

Elena said, "I'm kind of doing both right now."

Dave said, "Problem is, what to do now? If you pissed off this lizard guy personally, and they've got a hit out on you, they're not gonna just give up and go away. The narco networks are global, and certainly Mexico and the USA won't be safe for you unless you can get into something like the witness protection program."

Elena said, "I looked into that, but I don't actually know anything that is not publicly available information, so I would never qualify for it. They don't spend money to protect journalists."

The food started arriving. We all sat back and watched while Camila and a busboy loaded plates onto the table.

I looked over at Mallory, sitting next to Elena. Her eyes were turned in my direction, but looking through me, not at me, like she was not seeing me. Mallory was locked into some kind of inner reflection. Gave me time to have a look at her. The head wasn't shaved, it was clean, like the hair had fallen out. I figured that was from the chemotherapy, or radiation, or whatever it was they had been trying on her. The L shape was just the skin flap over the cranial insertion. After a minute, Mallory focused and she saw me for the first time. Her gaze travelled up and we made eye contact. She smiled, and nodded to me, like she knew something, like we had a secret. I found myself nodding back, without really knowing what I was nodding for. Mallory looked like she'd made a decision, or come to a conclusion about something. What, I didn't know.

Mallory dropped her eyes and said, "Look at your hands Keeler, you disgusting man."

I looked at my hands, which were still filthy from digging around in the Desert Inn's ceiling. I hadn't cleaned them in the motel, like Elena had.

"Yeah ok." I got up, and adjusted the Glock at my back, stuck into the waistband. I glanced at Dave, who had noticed I was carrying. He looked back at his burger. I made my way across the restaurant toward the bathroom.

GETTING to the bathroom was not self-evident. I had to figure it out.

The Texas Roadhouse was divided into two areas, split by a partition wall that went up halfway to the ceiling. I was in one dining area, the bathrooms were in the other, across from the kitchen, visible through a service shelving unit where waiters and waitresses could receive plates of food as they were ready. I had to go all the way around, past the entrance, hooking around to a pair of swinging double doors at the end of the room. I shouldered the push plate into the mens room. Three sinks in a row, above it, three mirrors. I chose the middle section, looked in the mirror and saw my own dirty face looking back at me. I washed it, and washed my hands. Dried myself with a handful of paper towels, went back out into the restaurant.

The dining room was busy with people taking their meals apart, hungrily, with fork and knife and fingers. I moved through the corridor between tables, back toward the front. To get to our booth I would make a right at the glass doors, hooking back into the second dining area, and my T-bone steak. But a busboy got in my way. Right in front of the entrance doors. The kid was carrying a bucket of dirty dishes, gleaned from one of the tables. I had to skirt around him, like a little dance. I danced left, he danced to my right. I ended up against the entrance door, which opened out toward the parking lot. And in came the guy I had seen lying on the bed looking at Elena's phone, in room twelve of the Desert Inn.

We almost collided. He was shorter standing than he had looked lying on the motel bed. Thickly built, with a shaved head and wispy facial hair. I hadn't noticed the tattoo on the crown of his head. It was a dagger pointing down toward the nape of his neck. The tattoo below his chin was a bunch of large gothic letters. I would need to be standing below him to read them. The guy stepped aside at the last moment, and said, "Excuse me," which, with his accented English sounded like, 'accuse me.' He made eye contact, but there was no recognition in his dead and glossy eyes.

Which I found interesting.

I let the guy pass in front of me and watched as he moved into the dining area, searching the booths and tables. I pushed my hand around the back of my waist, under my t-shirt. Just resting it there, thumbs hooked into the belt loops, ready to take hold of the Glock if the guy did anything. So far, his hands were loosely hanging away from his sides. The guy was moving slowly, scanning faces. I could see our table from the entrance. Elena and Mallory were tucked into the booth with their backs to the door, facing the wall where Dave sat. The booth butting up against ours had a group of Texas sized people demolishing plates of barbecued ribs. As a consequence, I couldn't see Mallory at all, and only half of Elena's head. Dave faced the entrance, looking down at his plate, trying to get a handle on the burger.

The guy moved through to the back, and looked over. He saw Elena's profile, and then turned away to the other side, looked down at a phone, then back up. I watched him recognize her. The guy turned around quickly, like he'd decided something. I was not ready for the quick movement, and he would have caught me looking at him, but I got lucky, because Camila, the waitress, was between us and in the way. She dodged around him, diverting his attention for the half-second I needed. I used that half-second to snatch a menu from the pile by the cashier's desk and put my head down to read it. Two seconds later, the guy brushed past me, and out the door.

The guy had not recognized me. Which meant they didn't know me, yet. I figured they knew the rental car plate number and that was it.

I looked out the big windows to the parking lot. Across from the Texas Roadhouse restaurant, a pickup truck was parked tail in. It was a Japanese model with the same silhouette as the truck that had been watching the Desert Inn, narrow body and roof lights like evil rabbit ears. A couple of guys were hanging around in front of it. The guy I had just seen walked over to them.

I figured, if they didn't know me, they couldn't see me. I was invisible. I pushed through the front door and out into the heat. The Glock was tucked into my waistband, with a round in the chamber, ten in the magazine. Eleven rounds total, so how many guys was I going to have to think about?

I walked across the thoroughfare lane, past the pickup truck without staring. Truck was a Toyota with two guys sitting in the bed, two standing around on the asphalt. They looked like brothers, or cousins, or members of the same cult or gang. Tattoos, shaved heads, wispy facial hair, baggy t-shirts, cargo shorts and jeans. Other than that, they were built like anyone else, tall and short, skinny and fat, a cross section of the species. The short thickset guy with the dagger head tattoo was talking, and others were listening. The two guys from the Jeep Cherokee were missing, maybe out of the game.

For a moment I thought, maybe they were going to enter the restaurant and start blasting. If they moved in that direction, I would have to act.

I was doing calculations, four guys, eleven bullets. That's two bullets for each with a couple left over just in case. Not great, not terrible. Theoretically, I could just take them out right there and then. One each to the chest, real quick, then tap them in the head. It would be over inside of a minute. Plus, I could loot their weapons. But that logic belonged in Iraq or Syria, not the Walmart parking lot outside of Midland, Texas.

They didn't go anywhere. A big and tall guy with a facial tattoo of a bat across his eyes brought out his phone and started speaking into it. The short thickset guy with the dagger tattoo lit a cigarette. So, they were going to wait.

I figured I should do some reconnaissance, in case there were more of them. I walked into the row of parked cars, one over from the Toyota. There was a Chevy Caprice between me and the guys. The Chevy butted up against a Honda, and that was the row. I turned right at the feeder lane, around the back of the Honda, walking along the line of cars, checking each one for lurking assassins.

Nothing going on, nobody to see. Only normal citizens concerned with shopping, eating, or on their way to the movies. When I got to the end of the row, I made a sharp turn at the bigger thoroughfare lane, back to the other side of the parked cars, walking now in the direction of the Texas Roadhouse. So far so good.

As I came back to the restaurant, I spotted a second group, around fifty yards out, parked perpendicular to the restaurant entrance. The new sicarios were grouped around a big GMC sports utility vehicle. Two men standing, two women sitting on the lowered tailgate, swinging their legs. The women wore baseball caps and heavy makeup around the eyes. Sicarias, or cholas, female cartel assassins. Whatever, death does not discriminate. That brought the enemy count up to eight.

I thought, eleven rounds, six male sicarios, two female sicarias. Eight total. Doable, but sub-optimal.

I went back into the restaurant. Slid into the booth next to Dave, who was still involved with the complicated burger. I focused on the steak, which was still warm. I demolished it inside of two minutes, then started on the sides. Mallory was nibbling her burger, maybe a quarter eaten. Elena's plate was clean, and she was wiping it with a cornbread square from a basket that had appeared during my absence. Dave was holding his fingers above his plate, looking around for free napkins.

I said, "Dave, are you carrying?"

Dave said, "You bet."

"Mallory?"

"In the truck."

They both looked at me. I ate a waffle fry, and said, "Bumped into one of the guys from the motel, but he didn't make me. So, I went out and scouted. There's at least eight of them out there." I looked at Elena. "They have your picture, on their phones, the guy ID'd you."

She said, "In here?"

"I just watched him do it."

Mallory said, "No shit?"

I said, "Good thing is, they're in uniform, making themselves easy to identify."

Elena said, "Uniform?"

"Dressed up like Mexican gang bangers. Probably raided Walmart for out of season Halloween gangster costumes."

Dave said, "That's a good look. I was thinking of going for it myself come Halloween."

I looked over at him, the bushy white mustache and balding head with close cropped white hair. "No problem, all you need is to cut that mustache back a little, and get yourself a face tattoo of a mermaid."

"I'm not in the Marines. But, if you're going in that direction bud, I'd have a screaming eagle tattooed to my forehead."

Elena was looking at Dave and me in disbelief, she said, "You guys are crazy."

Mallory shook her head. "They're just being dumbasses. Cut it out Dad. Keeler, be serious for a minute."

So, I got down to brass tacks.

I SAID, "This is Texas. They can't know who's carrying, right? So, that's one reason they won't want to make a public scene."

Mallory said, "Everyone's carrying. I've got mine in the truck, but Dad doesn't go anywhere without his."

Dave said, "Smith & Wesson shorty forty, right here." He lifted his shirt and showed me the butt of a pistol, behind his hip.

I said, "We're a little low on firepower, compared to what I'm expecting these clowns to have. But we can be more accurate, and there are other ways to even it up. We need to choose our ground, and I don't want to lead them to your place, but maybe there's a spot you can think of?"

Mallory said, "Poppy Canyon." She looked at her father. "If we can get them bottlenecked in there, we'll pick them off from high ground. No way they can get out."

Dave said, "If they don't know the place. If they do, they won't fall for it."

"What's Poppy Canyon?"

Mallory said, "Down on 118. Part of the road dips into a place everyone calls Poppy Canyon. No lateral movement. Only vertical cliff face on either side. Lead vehicle blocks, trailing vehicle locks."

I said, "Worth a try, no reason to believe they're from here. Probably brought in from someplace else."

Mallory said, "San Antonio, or Fort Worth. If they're gang bangers."

Elena said, "Or Mexico."

Dave said, "No doubt they bring those guys in to do a hit, then run em back across to Mexico. Cartels are organized here."

I said, "Mallory, you keep a jerry can in the Bronco, with spare gas just in case?"

She nodded, "Yes, I do."

I said, "Of course you do. Finish up your cokes."

I drained my bottle of coke. They all looked at me for a moment, then tipped their own bottles.

Dave said, "Jesus Christ."

I got up from the table, and gathered the bottles together. Stuck all four fingers of my right hand into the little mouths of four empty glass coke bottles. I said, "I'm going to do a little DIY job. Won't take more than ten minutes. Why don't you guys order dessert, and coffee. I'll wait for you in the rental." I looked at Elena. "She goes with you in the Bronco." I jerked my thumb to the back, where the bathrooms and kitchen were. "And go out the back, through the kitchen. Nice and easy, no one's going to stop you. I'll clear the back-door, and pick you up at the Bronco."

Dave said, "And what if it all goes haywire?"

"I'll find you."

Mallory slid the keys to the Bronco across the table. She said, "Take a right, down by the movie theater."

I pocketed her keys, and said, "These will be on the rear left tire."

Mallory nodded, "Got it."

Dave slid a zippo over, that went into my jeans as well.

Elena said, "Should we order you dessert?"

"Black Forest cake, to go, if they've got it."

I walked out.

The Toyota pickup truck was gone. I looked over to where the GMC sports utility vehicle had been, other side of a thoroughfare lane. Also gone. Which meant what? They had repositioned. I scanned the parking lot. The cars had thinned out some. Peak shopping time was over, with peak movie time replacing it.

First stop was the rental. I approached cautiously. People were parking and getting out of their cars, or doing the opposite, getting in their cars, and driving away. Not some kind of rush hour, more of a steady and relaxed early evening feeling. The night was hot, but a whole lot cooler than the murderous heat of the day. I couldn't see anyone watching the rental car, which did not mean they weren't. But I was also beyond caring about it. The situation was going in the other direction now. No more defensive action, worrying about what the enemy was doing. I was going to bring the worry right to them. Felt pretty good, and put a spring in my step.

My backpack was in the trunk of the Ford. So was the dirty white t-shirt I had replaced at Walmart. I dumped my stuff out of the backpack. There was not much in there to begin with. Toothbrush and a little tube of toothpaste. A Gore-Tex jacket for the rain. Extra t-shirt, underwear, and socks. My life in a bag. I put the coke bottles in, threw the roll of duct tape after them. Then I used the folding knife to tear off strips of the t-shirt. Four long lengths of torn cotton rag went in the backpack. I leaned into the passenger seat side at the front, took out the homemade cue ball sap from the glove compartment. The cue ball part of it fit perfectly in my front pocket, the ball bulging, and the handle stuck out a little for easy access.

Good to go.

The Bronco was parked by the movie theater. People on foot were choosing the narrower feeder lanes, which crossed thoroughfare lanes with two-way vehicular traffic.

It was definitely movie time. Moms and dads were walking alongside kids licking ice cream cones, finishing up buckets of popcorn, coming back from the movie to the family car, eyes wide from the spectacle and the sugar. Other family units were walking in the other direction, key fobs beeping, small children swinging between parents, dads carrying tired little toddlers. Groups of friends locked up their cars and moving toward the Multiplex. The scene could have been from a propaganda movie about America. The only thing missing was a squad of cheerleaders riding in the backseat of a convertible Mustang.

Mallory's key unlocked the back of the Bronco. She had two, five-gallon jerry cans in there, set into steel brackets. I put down my backpack, removed the coke bottles, and lined them up. Looked around to make sure that nobody was watching. I screwed a spout into the mouth of the jerry can, and filled the glass bottles three quarters up with gasoline. Not a drop spilled. I stuffed cotton strips into the bottles, making sure the rags fit tight into openings, so the gas wouldn't leak too badly. Then, tore off four strips of duct tape and used them to seal the coke bottle mouths, leaving enough room for the cotton strips to come out. Now I had four small Molotov cocktails standing on the lip of the Bronco's tailgate. Two rows of two bottles, stinking of gasoline, but not in danger of spilling. I taped two of the bottles together, and braided the cotton strips into a single wick. Did the same thing for the other two bottles. Now I had two decent petrol bombs that could do some damage.

The firepower issue was leveled up, to some degree. I packed the bombs into my backpack. Locked the Bronco, and put the keys on top of the left rear tire, under the wheel well.

I walked back to the Ford rental, thought about Black Forest cake. If it was in a to-go box, I wouldn't get the ice cream, which was ok. Nobody was following me. I did not see the Toyota pickup, or the GMC sports utility vehicle. The big lit up sign from the movie theater bounced off glossy car paint and was absorbed into the black asphalt. On the other side, the gas station was brilliantly lit. Red, white, and blue colors spilled out of the wrap-around roof sign. Stark white light from halogens lit the pumps below.

I turned the key in the ignition, the engine turned over. I moved the Ford out of the parking spot. Left along a row of cars, then another left down a feeder lane toward the restaurant. Right along the thoroughfare, then left around the Texas Roadhouse. No sign of the sicarios and sicarias, in either of their vehicles. The backside of the restaurant had a fenced in yard for the waste bins. I cruised past in one of the feeder lanes. Two parking lanes over from the restaurant. No evident watchers. I came back around and parked, about a hundred yards away. A couple minutes later, I saw Mallory, Elena, and Dave come out from the back. I let them go a while, watching to see if anyone was paying attention to them. I backed the Ford out of the spot, into the feeder lane, and followed the slight descent of the asphalt parking lot toward the movie theater complex, where Mallory had

parked the Bronco. I could still see their heads bobbing up
and down on the other side of the parked cars. I got to a
wide thoroughfare lane and paused at the stop sign to let a
family minivan pass.

Two small faces looked at me from the back seat of the minivan. A window decal said: 'Mom! Even when they're wrong,
they're right.'

I crossed the thoroughfare and continued down the feeder
lane. The cinema complex was immediately in front of me.
To the left, the Walmart store, two hundred yards away. To
the right, the exit to the street, maybe three hundred yards. I
scanned for my friends, having lost sight of them at the stop
sign. Then, I caught a glimpse of Elena. She had turned to
look around behind her. I thought maybe she'd looked at
me, but then she turned away again. At that moment, a
vehicle sped out of an empty parking spot just in front me,
and I hit the brake reflexively. It was the GMC sports utility
vehicle with the smoked windows. They had come through
an empty couple of spots.

I looked in the rearview and saw the silhouette of a Toyota
pickup truck, with roof lights making it look like an evil
rabbit. They had me cut off from the front, penned in from
the back.

TWO VEHICLES FRONT AND REAR, parked cars on the sides. I
was boxed in, with nowhere to go.

I could see nothing behind the GMC's tinted glass, only the
reflected gas station lights in red, white, and blue. The
Toyota behind me flicked on its high beams, and I looked

away from the rearview. I pulled my backpack from the passenger seat, opened the door, stepped out, and turned to the Toyota. I had my hands up and open, backpack on. A guy jumped down from the bed of the pickup truck. It was the big guy with the bat tattoo across his face. The bat wings covered his eyes, like theatrical makeup. He was holding a pistol, held low in front of him.

The guy stopped a couple of yards away. I could see him peering into the Ford, not finding what he was looking for. "Where's the girl?"

I said, "Did your mother abandon you? Are you still wondering why?"

"Where's the girl. Last chance."

"Before what?"

"Before I waste your ass." He worked the slide back on his pistol.

I said, "Take some advice. Get back in the truck, drive away."

The guy's lip trembled. "I told you last chance." He brought the gun up.

Instead of moving away, I took a step closer, because I did not think he wanted to shoot me. Not yet. The gun was another Glock. The muzzle square and ugly, with a barrel hole that looked right at me like a single eye.

I said, "You're pointing a gun at me. I tend to take that kind of thing personally."

"Man, who the fuck do you think you are, Mister wise ass? If I was in your position, I'd be on my knees begging to live."

"I bet you would."

Which made him even angrier. The face behind the bat tattoo had reddened, and the guy approached me with his gun pointed at my head. I was watching the trigger finger, curled inside the squared off guard. I wondered if I had been riding him too hard. And then, a staccato series of pops echoed out from the direction of the Multiplex. Six shots.

For two or three seconds, regular noises stopped as people paused.

I recognized the sound immediately: 5.56 NATO rounds out of an AR-15 rifle. The fire was semi-automatic, the shooter making one pull on the trigger for each shot. I looked up at the bat-faced guy, but he was looking over toward the Multiplex, where the shots had come from. I figured everyone else in the parking lot was doing the same thing.

The bat face guy had lost focus and I seized the moment. I stepped in to him, while ducking below the gun barrel. At the same time, my right hand was on the cue ball sap handle. Duct tape feeling smooth, but grippy with all that coiling. The guy grunted in surprise, and moved away instinctively, which pushed him off balance. His gun was moving down toward me again, which was not optimal. So, I twisted left and started to bring my right arm up with the cue ball sap. He got off a single shot, which blew past me, but dinged into the Ford rental like a bell being slapped. About an eighth of a second later, the duct taped cue ball slammed into his jaw, back around three inches from the chin.

Cue balls are half a gram heavier than the others balls on the pool table, the stripes, solids, and the eight ball. Six ounces, on average, which might not seem like much. But the mass of the ball itself gets multiplied by speed, and time. The mass of that cue ball, multiplied by the speed of my arm, and the time I had to unleash the blow, resulted in enough force to take out the guy's jaw bone, smashing right through it and snapping his head back. He dropped like a stone, and by the time his body hit the ground, I had picked up his fallen Glock. I slipped in between parked cars and ran toward the cinemas, head down.

I had told Dave that if everything went haywire, I would find them. And, everything was going haywire.

More shots were popping off, same weapon. Another sequence of five rounds. No return fire from Dave's shorty forty, which was concerning. A one-sided attack. Shooter with an AR-15 rifle, firing NATO rounds. The back of my mind registered ten so far. AR-15 magazines usually take thirty rounds. Twenty to go before the shooter had to change magazines.

The back of my mind said, twenty rounds is enough. The front of my mind was registering the growing panic around me.

First, it was a woman hustling kids in front of her. A responsible parent who maybe heard gunshots and was getting her kids to the minivan, getting the hell out of there, and perhaps stopping by a food franchise drive-thru on the way home. Other people were just looking around curiously, too cool to panic. I passed a couple of young guys with their girlfriends. They both had stupid grins on their faces, while the girls were not embarrassed to be worried. Which made sense, if you consider that teenage girls are often more sensible than boys their own age. One of the guys had a baseball hat on backward. He said, "What is that, like a gun?" The other guy gazed around mute, grinning.

I went on down the feeder lane toward the cinema, holding the looted Glock against my leg, and ran into Mallory, Dave, and Elena huddled between the Bronco and another car.

I said, "Who's shooting at you?"

Mallory said, "Nobody's shooting at us. I thought it was you getting shot at."

I shook my head. "Nobody shot at me, yet. I got boxed in by them. I used the shots as cover to get away."

Three more shots were fired, and I popped my head up to look. The fire was coming from the direction of the parking lot exit. Another shot. Screams. A stampede of panicked running.

I said, "Fire is coming from among the parked cars." A man was dragging a boy by the hand, walking fast, like he was trying not to break into a run so his son wouldn't see dad panicking. I halted him. "Did you see what's going on?"

The guy was breathing heavily, he said, "Someone got out of his car and started shooting people. Get the hell out of here." He dragged his son away.

Mallory shook her head, and said, "Active shooter. On top of everything else."

Another volley of five gunshots from the shooter. People were streaming away from the source. I got down and looked under the cars. There was a body down, about twenty yards away. Closer in, I saw a woman huddling behind a Range Rover, stabbing at her phone. There would be a dozen people doing exactly the same thing. The police would start to arrive soon, minutes away.

I figured, like in every crisis there was an opportunity here.

I said, "We're going to have to respond. Dave and Mallory, you need to direct people to a secure location. We don't want them crossing the shooter's line of fire, so move them along the wall and into the Walmart. Looks like he's among the parked cars, but that may change if he's mobile."

Mallory said, "What about the people trying to kill Elena, aren't we worrying about them?"

I said, "They're not going to stop hunting us just because of this FUBAR situation. So, I'm going to take them out, use the confusion."

Dave said, "What about shutting down the shooter?"

"I'm going to try both at the same time."

I was looking around the parking lot, tracking the vehicles. There was confusion and cars blocking other cars, as folks started trying to get out of there. I climbed up on the hood of the closest car. It gave me height and I was able to see the Toyota stuck in a feeder lane about fifty yards away, toward the Walmart. The GMC was higher up the incline, in a thoroughfare lane by the gas station, covering the exits. There wasn't anyone in the bed of the Toyota truck. I had put the bat faced guy down, but there had been four total in the Toyota, which meant at least two of them were on foot. Made sense. One or two guys in the car, the others on foot either side, trawling through the parking lot, searching.

I jumped down again, and pointed two fingers at Dave and Mallory. "You two get the civilians safe, then take the Bronco and wait for me up by the gas station. They don't know you yet, or the vehicle, so better to keep it that way if we can. There's a hostile GMC sports utility vehicle up there filled with bad guys, smoked windows. Stay away for now."

Mallory sprang up. "Come on Dad." I watched her stride out into the open, and use that commanding Lieutenant Colonel's voice. "Folks, we need to get you safe. The safest place is the Walmart. We need to get there by moving in single file against the building. Now."

Dave was already finding civilians huddled down behind whatever cover they had been able to reach, corralling them toward the building.

I looked at Elena, "Good to go?"

Elena brushed the hair out of her eyes, "Good. Yes. You seem to be the expert."

I held the Glock taken from the guy with the bat tattoo for Elena. "Know how to use this?"

"I've fired one a few times, what else is there to know?"

"Not much. Just don't point it at anyone you're not planning on shooting."

I checked the load, full magazine, one in the chamber. Gave her the gun, and took the other one out of my waistband.

I LOOKED OVER THE CARS. The Toyota pickup truck had gotten out of the jam, and was moving our way. I could not see the entire truck, but the distinctive roof lights were moving above the parked cars. I was unable to see the foot soldiers out on the flanks, who I figured were keeping low, like we were.

I said to Elena, "Like before at the motel, we move as a unit, keep in touch." She nodded. I moved in a crouch between cars, toward the Toyota. I remembered a briefing about active shooters. Average police response time is five or six minutes. Usually the shooter commits suicide, or is killed by the police.

Sirens were already faintly audible in the distance.

Elena was holding on to my backpack, shadowing me. I squatted down and paused, "Open the backpack and take a look." I waited while she undid the clasp, looked inside, and was able to see the coke bottles taped together, filled with gas. "You see them?"

"I see them. Should I take one out?"

"Not yet." I gave her Dave's zippo. "When I say so, you take one out, hand it off to me. Think you can do that?"

She said, "Do I light it?"

"I'll tell you when to light it. You just hand it to me. Okay?"

Another nod. "I think so."

"Good. And keep the gun down until you need to use it."

Elena nodded again. "You already said that."

"I know. But it's a point worth repeating."

She nodded for the third time. "Okay."

Elena was doing well, under the circumstances. There were three more shots. The back of my mind had lost count. The front of my mind said it did not matter at that point.

We moved out, weaving between cars in the direction I had last seen the Toyota truck. A middle-aged man snuck around the corner of a VW van. I did not blink, kept the Glock down behind my leg and kept moving. Not too fast, not too slow. The guy brushed past me, his eyes bugging. I crossed over past the van, squeezing between the hood of a red Hyundai and a Chevy. Movement to my right. A man appeared around the back of the Hyundai. I saw him spot us, and raise his gun hand. I had the Glock up, put two into his chest. Bang, bang.

The guy went down on his back, floundering, like he was trying to get up, but couldn't figure out how to make that work. He squeezed the trigger wildly, twice. One of the rounds went into the sky. The other came off at a shallow angle, with the muzzle pointed low at the car. I ducked my head away. The bullet hit the Hyundai's underbody from a foot away, ricocheted back into the ground, and smacked into the bumper of the next car over. The guy tried to get the gun up again, but I moved in, one quick step, and put a round into his face, a red hole bloomed under his right eye. The head snapped back to the asphalt. The guy settled into death with a grimace.

I peered through the Hyundai's windshield. The Toyota pickup was a couple of car lengths away. I turned to Elena. "Now." I crouched down, my back to Elena, allowing her to fiddle around inside the bag. I looked over my shoulder. I would not have much time with the improvised bomb. I looked up again through the windshield. I figured it would be better if we were further up, at an angle that would allow me to put the bomb right into the cab. Elena handed the taped coke bottles to me. I took the bottles, and hustled along in a crab walk, keeping real low. Elena was right behind me. We got three cars over, and I switched the Glock to my left hand and said, "Light it."

Elena concentrated. The zippo clicked again, I felt the heat as the braided shirt strips flamed. I moved quickly between the two cars, timing it just right as the Toyota came abreast. I saw the short thickset guy driving, window down, eyes scanning. Next to him, on the other side of the Toyota, the guy with the bat tattoo who's jaw I had destroyed, was slumped against the door. The driver caught a glimpse of me just as I was winding up. He acted fast, and hit the gas. But I got the bomb off in time. Watched it sailing through the air, making an arc of fire right into his window. The flaming coke bottle dinged off the steering wheel, and impacted on the toughened glass of the Toyota's windshield. The pickup truck's cab blossomed into flame, with a rushing sound, as combustible gasoline splashed everywhere. I caught a glimpse of the short thickset guy's upper body and head, on fire. On the other side of him the bat tattoo guy was shuddering, burning gas all over him. Then, the truck was accelerating up the thoroughfare lane, as if the driver's foot was glued to the pedal.

Two shots popped from only a car's length away. The driver's side window of the Hyundai was punctured inches from my head. Two holes in the tempered, laminated glass. No shattering, but I got a face full of glass powder, which was not pleasant, but thankfully did not get in my eyes. While my head was down dealing with that, I heard three shots in quick succession from behind me. I wheeled around, and there was Elena, her back to me. Ten feet in front of her, a guy was face down, half underneath a car, looking dead. She stepped to him and put a round into his head.

I said, "That's how you do it."

I put a hand on Elena's shoulder. Keeping her down with me behind the car. I counted enemies. Three down from the Toyota pickup truck, including the thickset short guy who had been driving. The guy with the bat face tattoo would not be rejoining the fight, which accounted for all four of them. I stood up from behind the car, looked back toward the Walmart. A line of civilians was hustling along the wall in a half crouch. I could make out Mallory's pale bald head at the rear, pushing them along single file. Dave was out on the wing with his bushy white mustache and military haircut. Fine, but something was bothering me and I did not know what.

Elena was looking at me. She looked tense. I said, "Give me a second. I'm thinking. Don't forget to breathe."

She started breathing. The tension in her face washed out, like a blanket being straightened. Elena shifted her body closer to me and leaned an elbow on my shoulder. I hadn't heard any more shooting from the gunman with the AR-15. I said, "You see anything moving, you tell me."

Police sirens were wailing, closer than before, multiplied and coming from all directions.

Around us now, nothing moved. Nobody was running. It looked as if everyone had gone to cover hiding, either to the Walmart with Mallory and Dave, or on their own, huddled under cars, or behind whatever obstacles they could find.

Hoping that the shooter would not find them. I turned toward the gas station, up the slight incline. The GMC sports utility vehicle was stationary. The windows were dark. No way of knowing how many were in there.

Elena said, "I don't see anything. Maybe it's over."

I said, "Maybe. Maybe not."

I rewound the situation for a second, put myself in the shoes of my enemy. What would I be doing if I were them? For one thing, I would not have four men sitting in a vehicle covering exit routes. Two guys sitting in the GMC would be enough. The other two could be mobile, out hunting on foot. That's what had been nagging at me. About a quarter of a second after that thought occurred to me, I heard a bang, and was pounded in the side by a giant metal fist.

It was a bullet, not a fist. It smacked into my right side, rib cage area. I felt the impact in my ears, like my bone structure had been rocked. I have been shot before, which did not make this time any better. What happens is, you do not realize you've been shot, because there is no pain at first. You feel as if you've been hit with a hammer, which in a way you have. The shot blew me off balance, tossing me against the side panel of a parked car. The Glock went skitting away under the car. What I felt was winded, like the breath had been sucked out of me. I looked up at Elena. She was looking at me, horrified. Then she turned back around. Behind her I saw a woman approaching, pistol held out in front. It was one of the sicarias I had seen in the back of the GMC.

∼

THE SICARIA WORE a tank top exposing a firm muscled belly with a tattooed tiger jumping out of her denim shorts. Up top she had yanked her hair into a severe ponytail, which stretched her manicured eyebrows toward the hairline. The sicaria laughed hoarsely, and shouted over her shoulder in Spanish. A man stepped into view behind her. He had a wispy mustache, with long hairs sticking out, like a cat's whiskers. The guy said something in return. I could not understand the language. The woman made a sound, like kissing her teeth. The man kissed his teeth back at her. He pushed his gun into the front of his pants, and pulled a phone from his pocket. When he brought the phone up, I understood the teeth kissing language. They were going to film Elena's execution, and probably mine for good measure. Maybe they needed proof for the boss, El Lagarto.

One of them needed to hold the phone, the other one got to be in the movie with the gun, for the boss to see. The sicaria had won, no contest really. I got over the shock of being shot. My right side felt heavy, and would have needed immediate attention. But I was still alive, and none of that would matter in a second or two, because we were about to be executed on camera. I was down next to the car, and reached my right arm under it, without looking, hoping to find the gun that had been knocked out of my hand.

The guy said something in Spanish. I made out the word *filmado*. He was filming. The sicaria smiled to the camera, and theatrically chambered a round in her Glock. She turned to Elena and extended her arms to shoot, holding the gun with both hands. I felt the gun under the car with the tip of my fingers. I managed to bring it closer to where I could get a grip on it. I was not in pain from being shot, feeling only dull pressure and a sting.

I might have reached the gun, but there is no way to know, because two shots popped then, and the tattooed tiger on the sicaria's belly exploded in a flash of gore and blood. She looked surprised, and flopped forward. Her knees folded under her weight and she fell on her face, one arm still outstretched, the other crumpled under her body. The guy holding the phone to film was still looking at the screen, as if unable to decide if his life was happening inside of that rectangle, or out here in the real world.

Another shot cracked from nearby, bringing him back to reality. The bullet came from a three-quarter angle behind him, and entered his cheek. The projectile passed through his head, probably bouncing around in there, spinning at high speed, and exited the other side of his head, pulping his ear. Dead on arrival.

Elena screamed. She had the sicaria's blood all over her face. I pushed her behind me, and saw the shooter walking toward us. It was Caleb. He was wearing the same red polo shirt with the Dale's Oilfield Supply logo in white at his breast. It was the logo of the company he'd been fired from in the morning. Caleb was holding an AR-15 style assault rifle across his body. I had seen him denied at the Walmart, but someone had sold him the rifle anyway. The gun looked like a budget version, with impactful detailing designed to impress. Maybe he'd picked it up in a private sale from someone he knew.

Caleb crossed the feeder lane. He walked lethargically, dragging unlaced construction boots. His face was drawn, like he had aged a decade between breakfast and now. I wondered if giving him two dollars that morning would make an impression, if it would prevent him from shooting us, or if he had become an automaton, his mind tipped over the edge and he was just going to shoot anyone he could find. Caleb pulled the assault rifle to his thick shoulder. The barrel pointed at me, and we made eye contact over the gunsights.

I had my hands down at my sides, palms up. I considered the comparative advantages and disadvantages of direct eye contact. I am no psychologist, but I once read an article in a dentist office waiting room, about gorillas. You are not supposed to look directly at the silverback alpha male, because he will try and kill you. Apparently, eye contact is a challenge to supremacy for gorillas. But then again, Caleb wasn't a gorilla, or an alpha male. Deep down he was just a weak guy. And I had helped him buy his breakfast burrito, which might count for something, or not. Caleb advanced, staring at me expressionlessly over the gunsight.

I said, "Sausage *and* Bacon, no coffee. You don't drink coffee because it interferes with your meds."

I broke eye contact, looked at his trigger finger. It was out of the trigger guard and pointed at me. I shifted to his eyes, and re-engaged. He broke off the eye contact, turned away and walked toward the Multiplex entrance.

I scraped the Glock from under the car, and came up, steadying the gun over the hood of the vehicle next to us. I put a bullet into the back of Caleb's right thigh, and he went down. The first two police cars were screaming to a stop. Car doors slamming open. Caleb was mute, and scrambling to bring his AR-15 up. The police lights swept across the lot, isolating him against the dark asphalt. The cops did not wait to see what would happen next, they opened up. A volley of rifle and pistol fire in multiple calibers crackled like static electricity. Caleb's body shuddered as it was riddled with bullets. Behind him, stray rounds raised cement dust where they impacted dirt, asphalt, and the concrete wall of the Multiplex.

I pulled the backpack off. Found the duct tape. Pulled up my t-shirt. Elena did not need to be asked, she took the tape from me and tore off a strip. "Will this be enough?"

I inspected the wound and nodded. The bullet had not entered my body. It had broken skin and glanced off my rib, which was probably cracked. There was bleeding, but it looked worse than it was. I guided her hand to the spot where I had been hit. "Press hard. Use two strips."

She pressed hard, grunting with the effort. Her hair covered my face for a moment, and I felt the closeness of her skin. She tore off another strip of tape. When she was finished, Elena moved back, heat going with her. Something glittered on the asphalt. I picked it up and held a small piece of metal in my palm. Elena said, "What is that?"

I said, "It's the bullet that hit me."

"What?"

"It deflected off my rib and then hit the car door. Here." I pointed to where the round had hit the car and put a little dimple in the metal, flaking off paint.

She said, "That's amazing." I wasn't going to argue, that would have been painful with a cracked rib.

The air was all dry heat and cop radio noise. Flashing blue lights bounced off the movie complex walls. Right in front of us, the sicaria groaned and moved. Her buddy was dead, staring sightlessly into the asphalt, but not her. I moved over the sicaria's body and inspected the damage. Caleb had fired twice, but only one round had hit. Looked like it had gone in through the small of her back, but the damage had been done when the bullet exited her inguinal region. Blood was pooling below her. She had lost a lot of blood already. Combat medic's dilemma. Do you save the enemy's life when they're wounded? The answer is, it depends. Police were all around, so the fight was over for now.

I took out the knife and started cutting her shorts off. The sicaria was bleeding from a severed femoral artery in her groin, a junctional hemorrhage. A tourniquet was not going to work. I figured the best I was going to do was to cut my way through the ligaments, fat, and muscle to expose the artery, then clamp it between my thumb and forefinger. I would wait until an ambulance arrived, which was going to be very soon.

A male voice shouted in my ear, "Put your hands in the air." The voice was hoarse with panic. I looked up at a uniformed policeman, a round man with a smooth red face and light thinning hair. The cop was pointing his gun at me.

I said, "I'm a medic. She's bleeding out."

The cop was shaking. He stared for several seconds, and moved away.

I sliced through the denim of her shorts, and peeled the blood-soaked fabric away from her skin. I could feel something rectangular and stiff in the front pocket. Too thin, and pliable to be a phone. The exit wound was at the junction of her right leg and the torso, at the inguinal crease. The sicaria was listless and moaning, bleeding to death. Arterial blood was spreading into the asphalt under her body, finding its way into cracks and grooves. Cutting down on the fabric, I brushed up against whatever was in her pocket again, and realized what it might be. I stopped trying to help her, wiped bloody fingers on her jeans, and slid them into the sicaria's pocket.

I pulled out a passport. Dark green, a gold embossed logo of an eagle eating a snake, and the word 'Mexico' in large gold letters. I looked at Elena's shocked and bloody face, right beside mine.

"You have any identification on you?" She nodded. I said, "Give it to me. Right now."

Elena fumbled the button of her jeans and peeled the top of them down, revealing her money belt. She unzipped the document holder, fished inside and handed me a worn Mexican passport. Otherwise identical, except for what was inside. I opened it and saw Elena's photo, which had been taken maybe ten years earlier. The name in her passport was Jolene Teresa Medina Cordero. Complicated name, but none of it said Elena. I looked at Elena and said, "This is you?"

She nodded. It was not the moment to discuss identity. I slid her passport into the dying woman's pocket. The sicaria's document went in my pants pocket.

The sicaria was not going to live, and maybe Elena's identity could die with her. I pictured the obituary section, the day after a mass shooting event. One of the lines would read: 'Jolene Teresa Medina Cordero, Mexican National'. If the sicaria had come over the border illegally, it would work. El Lagarto would be paying attention, that was for damn sure. I scooted over and took the phone out of the dead guy's clenched fingers.

The screen was still illuminated. The phone was recording. I pressed a red button with a square on it, and the recording stopped. A green button showed up with the word *Enviar*. I showed it to Elena. She said, "You want to send that?"

I said, "No. Delete it."

She huddled over the phone and pressed some buttons. She said, "He was going to send the video."

I said, "Wait." Pointed over between the two cars. "Give me that, and go lie down and look dead."

Elena got the idea immediately. She lay down on the asphalt and played dead. She did it well, open eyes, face bloodied with the sicaria's spray. I snapped a shot. The green button appeared again with the word *Enviar*, and I tapped it with my forefinger.

I said, "Done." I looked at Elena. She looked at me, her eyes wide. I nodded, and she nodded back. It would not do for the sicaria to accidentally live, so I waited for her to die. She had hair the same color as Elena's, and she was twenty years younger. It took three more minutes for death to take her.

THE PLACE WAS SOON SWARMING with police and media. Television trucks eventually arrived, from big cities like Dallas–Fort Worth, and smaller cities like San Antonio, and Albuquerque. Local people drove slowly by, rubbernecking all that activity.

By then we were gone.

After the sicaria was confirmed dead, I cleaned myself as best as I could, given the circumstances. Neither Dave nor Mallory had fired a shot, so I did not have to worry about the casings. I wiped the two Glocks down and left them with the bodies. Better than having them with us. With all that law enforcement, I wasn't surprised to find that the GMC sports utility vehicle was no longer around. I figured the remaining two sicarios would want to high tail it across the border, soon as they could. The sicario's phone stayed in my pocket, destined to be crushed.

Dave and Mallory went first in the Bronco, we followed.

Once we were away from the Walmart complex and cruising on route 118, I turned to look at Elena. She was curled against the passenger door, looking at the night. The desert was a thin black horizon, a shade lighter in the sky than the earth. Mostly a straight line, with some hills once in a while. The electric lights out there were sparse.

I said, "So is it Jolene, or Elena?"

She did not say anything, just kept on looking out at the night. After a while she said, "Jolene."

I said nothing.

"I'm sorry I lied to you."

I said, "What else did you lie about?"

"I went to school for journalism, but I never worked as a journalist. Other than that, the basics are the same." She shifted to face me. "I was his girlfriend, not a journalist. His wife decided to have me killed. So now you tell me, would you have helped me if I had told you that in the beginning?"

I said, "It wouldn't have made any difference to me, but I understand why you would change the story. Some people might have judged you, morally. His wife found out, and she wanted you dead. So, the hit on you is from her, not the lizard guy, El Lagarto, who is in fact your boyfriend."

She said, "Not any more he isn't. You should understand that I was not a complete victim. Being his mistress for ten years had benefits, even if in the beginning I didn't get to make a choice."

"How did you meet him?"

"Working in a nightclub. He decided he wanted me, like a shopping trip. One night he was there looking at me, the next day two of his guys came and told me to pack up my things, he wanted me."

"Just like that."

"Just like that."

I said, "Ten years is a long time, I guess it wasn't all that bad."

"I had it good, compared to most people's lives. After a while I wasn't a prisoner, and he's a smart guy, but limited, in terms of his interests."

"Why did his wife suddenly care?"

She said, "He stopped seeing her. I think he got bored with her after they had kids. She was a beauty queen when he married her. By the end it was more like I was his wife and she was just stale bread. So, after ten years, that psychopath decided that she wanted me dead, and he just rolled over and let it happen."

I said, "Mother of his children, and all that."

"Right."

"What's the wife's name?"

She laughed, and said, "Elena."

"So, what am I supposed to call you now, Jolene?"

"Call me Jo."

I tried it out, "Jo." Felt okay saying it.

Jo looked at me and smiled. She said, "If this weren't some dumb modern car, I would come over there and give you a hug. But if I did that, the seat belt thing would beep right?"

I said, "Who cares, give me a hug."

Jo unclipped the seat belt, scooted over, and rested her head on my chest. She wrapped her left arm around my neck. The fingers of her right hand rested lightly on my forearm. She said, "A decent guy is hard to find."

I said nothing, enjoying the feeling of her pressed against me. The seat belt warning beeped, but it kept me awake.

AN HOUR LATER, I carried Mallory into the ranch house. She was having a bad spell. It had started in the Walmart parking lot, and gotten worse during the car ride back. I laid her down on the couch. Dave had a routine going, with pain medication and ways to alleviate symptoms of nausea. This bad spell was not something new. They were coming more frequently now than in previous weeks. The ranch house had two guest rooms with en suite bathrooms and shower facilities. Jo went into one of them, I got the other.

I threw my backpack on an armchair in the room. Peeled off my clothes and kicked them in a corner. Then I got in the shower. I let the hot water stream over the top of my head and the nape of my neck. It felt really good. I soaped myself and watched the dirty, bloody residue come off and swirl into the drain with the centrifugal force. I toweled off, and felt human again. The house was quiet, the bedsheets were clean. Through the open window, the night sky was scattered with bright stars. It was cool now, this late. I slipped into bed, stretched out, and was asleep pretty much instantly.

THE HOUSE SMELLED like bacon and coffee. The two best things in the world, after the best thing in the world. I felt full of energy, well rested and relaxed. I showered again. My clothes needed to be washed, or burned, but the jeans were almost acceptable and I had an extra t-shirt and underclothes in the rental.

Dave was sitting at the table looking at a laptop computer. He pointed at the kitchen area. "Self-service. Don't make a mess."

I said, "Yes sir."

I found a pile of plates on the counter, and a large skillet on the stove. The skillet contained bacon and scrambled eggs, one pile next to the other. Sliced bread was on a cutting board by the toaster. A butter dish was out, and jelly in a jar. A pitcher of freshly made coffee and cups to pour it in were right there on the table, for easy access. I loaded up with bacon and eggs.

Dave was looking at the news. I set my plate down and pulled out a chair. He said, "You want to hear it?"

I said, "Sure."

He'd gleaned the useful information, separated it from the rest, and summarized. "Looks like twelve dead. Five of them Mexican nationals. Fifteen injured, some critically, so the death count may rise. How many did you bag yourself?"

I said, "Shot two or three, burned two to death. Another two got shot by the crazy guy, Caleb. Kind of did me a favor."

Dave was looking at me with his head tilted slightly. He said, "Not bad for today's army."

"Air Force."

He turned back to the computer. "The burned pickup truck is being attributed to the shooter, no details on that, just journalists speculating. But the FBI did come in with a forensic unit."

I said, "They give out any useful information?"

"None from the FBI, but all kinds from nosy reporters." He turned the computer around and showed it to me. The article said they'd found 5.56 caliber NATO rounds mixed up with assorted calibers from law enforcement, and a 9mm Smith & Wesson that Caleb had been carrying, along with his AR-15 copy."

I shrugged. The FBI was not going to miss any details. The parking lot was going to be blocked off and divided into a grid. A team of highly trained and experienced investigators would comb through that grid with white suits and rubber gloves. Everything not nailed down would get bagged and taken to forensic examination. For projectile trajectories they would come in with laser scanners and range finders. The wind resistance and humidity would be measured, and used to calculate each bullet's precise trajectory. All of that was going to get modeled in a computer, and then poured over by a team of nerds. There was no chance that they would miss the fact that three of the dead were killed by 9mm rounds at close range, away from the other shootings, and that two had been burned to death by coke bottle Molotov cocktails. But they weren't going to volunteer their unanswered questions either. The Feds tend to keep those to themselves and relentlessly pursue the investigation, no matter how long it takes.

I said, "So they're keeping the burned guys to themselves. Don't blame them, since they have no answers. No doubt they will figure out the narco connection, which will puzzle them for about ten years. Publicly, they will lump it in with everything else."

Dave said, "Most likely. It's not like they're going to give information to the narcos for free."

I said, "They release names?"

Dave said, "Not officially. But names are coming out unofficially, on blogs and social media accounts. It's impossible to stop it. Look at this." He switched windows on his web browser and pointed to a list of casualty names. "Doesn't say if they're dead or injured, but someone leaked. Didn't find any Elena on the list."

I scrolled down and found Jolene Teresa Medina Cordero.

I put my finger on the name and said, "Turns out her name's not Elena, it's Jolene. So, we know that one's dead. I verified it."

Dave said, "Jolene huh? Like the Dolly Parton song."

I said, "Call her Jo."

Dave shrugged, we exchanged pleased looks. I poured a cup of coffee. It was excellent.

Through the glass doors, I could see the oak trees that Mallory had marked out for her final resting place. I left Dave to his research and stepped out onto a wide deck. It was still early, and not yet scorching hot. There was even a cool breeze. I stretched and cracked my joints.

The stand of oaks was planted at the foot of rolling hills on the other side of a big horse pen. It was a large group of trees, widely distributed to make room for long branches that swept almost to the ground. I had read about oak stands, how underground the roots are all connected, like a family. And they talk to each other somehow, in the language of nutrients, with the help of subterranean funguses. A half dozen old trees were spread out below the hills. Here in West Texas they grow low and wide, as if to go any higher would just dry them out more than was necessary. The powerful boughs branched off low enough that I leaned my arms in the junction of one of them, where bough meets trunk. The air smelled of manure and grass, and I figured that the trees were old enough to have been planted by the first optimistic settlers. They must have been optimists, because back then as now, this was frontier territory, and only the toughest survived.

The sun was coming up over the hills. On the other side was the ranch house. The sun would go down behind that.

Mallory walked over in bare feet and jeans. She said, "You like the spot?"

I said, "Smells nice."

"No oil to drill for down here, so we are safe from that, pretty much forever."

I did not ask her how she was feeling, because I figured she was feeling bad. But it would be impolite to ignore the elephant in the room.

I said, "How do you prepare for death, mentally. Must be a challenge."

She said, "You can't prepare for it. I don't think anyone can."

"So, you just live with it there, like right there next to you, breathing over your shoulder, all the time."

"You know what that's like Keeler."

I said, "Not the same. This is a sure thing."

Mallory shrugged and brushed her foot against the rough bark. "You ever see that old Ingmar Bergman movie about death?"

I shook my head.

Mallory said, "I've had plenty of time to watch TV recently. Saw it late one night. The movie is about a guy who comes back from a middle eastern war. Time wise, we're talking the Middle Ages and the Crusades. Guy gets back to Sweden and death is there waiting for him. Like, he survived all those tours, and comes back only to find death waiting at home. It's in the time of the plague and everything. So, the guy makes a deal with death, tries to negotiate."

"And death lets him go?"

"No. The guy challenges death to a game of chess. In the end he loses the game and death takes him away, but in the meantime he's distracted death long enough to save a couple of people. Death is pissed, but nothing he can do."

I said, "Tactical delay. Magnificent. So, how are you going to distract death?"

Mallory looked up at me, with a twinkle in her eye. "I feel like I already have." She walked over to one of the oaks. It had roots rippling out of the stony ground. "This is the one. I'm going to be buried right here." She traced a rectangle with her toe. "My body will be buried here, but I'll live on out there, cheating death."

I said, "How do you figure that?"

"Elena's dead, right?"

"Officially speaking, in terms of bureaucracies and narco cartel accounting, I hope so."

"So, what's she going to do now, walk around like a ghost? No. She's going to get a new name with a new identity."

I said, "You want Elena to replace you."

Mallory said, "That's right. She's going to replace me."

"What about the doctors and everyone up at the VA hospital."

"I thought about that. I've already stopped cooperating with the doctors."

"You think that will work? They won't come after you?"

She said, "They're sick of me, believe me, I'm a pain in the ass."

I said nothing.

Mallory punched me in the arm. "C'mon, what do you think Keeler?"

"I think it's an outstanding plan."

Mallory beamed with happiness. "Thank you. I think so too."

"But her name's not Elena, and the whole journalist story was hooey."

"Yeah, no shit. What is she really, a Mexican cop?"

"El Lagarto's mistress. Wife got jealous and put out a hit."

Mallory's eyes twinkled and her mouth turned up in an amused grin. "Outstanding."

We looked over at the ranch house. Perfect timing. Jo was setting down her breakfast plate. She and Dave were talking. She glanced at us through the glass doors, smiled, and raised her hand, wiggling the fingers. We waved back at her.

An extract from the first full-length Tom Keeler novel

STRAIGHT SHOT

A man was walking the platform, scanning the train as it crept into Alencourt station. I was sitting at the window, watching him as we got closer. The brakes shrieked. The guy moved slow and stiff, his head swiveling like a searchlight as the train inched past. Looking for someone. He walked against the train's direction, while his head rotated back with it, holding each window in place as his eyes examined it, then circling back to scan again, as the next car came abreast.

The train approached; we got closer. I could see his eyes darting around, while the head moved smoothly. Then the eyes found me, but settled below my eye line. Like he wasn't interested in my face. Then the guy lifted his gaze to mine and we were looking directly at each other, engaged. The train was moving painfully slow, so there was plenty of time to get a good look.

Looked like he had recognized me, but I didn't know him.

Then the train stopped with a delayed lurch, and I saw him back off and disengage. Around me passengers were already dragging their bags and children off luggage racks and train seats. Soon they were flooding the platform and the guy was gone.

I was halfway to the entrance hall before I saw him again, over by the ticket desk, trying not to stare at me. He was maybe nineteen or twenty. Close small eyes and a tiny chin, like a rat. Dark hair buzzed to a number two, stripes shaved into one side. Like the Adidas logo. I went over to the information board and examined him in the glass reflection. He couldn't stop himself from looking at me. Not a professional. Some kind of petty criminal maybe.

I looked up at the clock over the information booth. Quarter to noon, Saturday, June 23rd. It was my first time in France.

The station was busy. People dragged wheeled suitcases around, ran for trains. Footsteps slapped on the concrete, echoing around the big hall. Mothers and Fathers pulled their kids. The rat-faced guy I'd never seen before was just standing there looking at my back. I supposed he was planning to mug me.

The entrance to the street was a wide stone arch leading to two-way traffic and a park on the other side. There was a kiosk in the park with newspapers and magazines and a big coffee cup on the roof. I figured I could cross through the traffic and wait to see if the guy came after me. On top of that I could get a cup of coffee.

I jogged across, weaving between taxis.

I ordered coffee at the kiosk and watched the entrance to the train station. Nobody came, nothing happened. I stretched out and yawned. My joints cracked. Twelve hours on the train. The coffee was dark and bitter. It came in a small paper cup. I drank it in two sips, crushed the cup in my fist and threw it into a garbage can. I didn't see anyone coming after me.

The weather was grey and so was the town. Grey stone. Poured concrete fixtures. Warm droplets of moisture hung in the air, threatening rain.

I noticed the second guy right off the bat. He must have circled around the park to flank me. This guy was bigger than rat-face and wore jeans with a thin leather jacket. He looked like a young thug. Same age as the first guy. The second one had wet looking hair combed in a side part.

So I figured the first guy would be coming up behind me. They had wanted me to notice the second one. That was the strategy, distract, induce panic, come at me from both sides. I'd been out of the military for only a week. Their little strategy wasn't going to work.

The park was carved up into little walk-ways. I went off the footpath and cut across the lawn. Using peripheral vision, I clocked rat-face coming off the street and passing the kiosk. He and his leather jacket buddy were moving in sync, wedging me in. Dense evergreens crowded the path where it sunk down in a dip a dozen yards away. The dip would do. I figured less than twenty seconds casual walking.

Laurel bushes blocked out the light. The dip was an inter-section. A spiderweb of narrow walkways converged in its hollow. But the two guys were gone. I stayed there for a couple of minutes to see if they would come. Maybe they were waiting me out. But nobody waits more than a minute. A minute's a long time if you're waiting. Young thugs in particular are impatient, nervous and jumpy. You can always wait them out. The two guys didn't show.

I exited the park and crossed over to the sidewalk. The town center was old and busy. The kind of old that gets preserved by committee. Busy with regular people doing regular things that hadn't changed all that much in a couple hundred years.

Twelve hours on the train made me want to stretch out. To walk. To loosen the hips and the knees and ankles. But first I wanted to stop by the town hall, see if I could find any record of my mother's family. She had been French, and spent her summers in Alencourt. I was curious about that side of my family because as far as I knew, my mother hadn't ever come back to France after moving to the United States.

The center of town was a big old medieval square with an ancient church right in the middle of it. The town hall was on the edge of the square. I told the old mustachioed guy at reception what I was looking for and he pointed across the square. He had to push his glasses down off his forehead to look at me. Blue eyes magnified and focused. He said that records were kept in the library, which was on the other side of the church. The old guy looked at his watch and shook his head, chances were the library was already closed for lunch.

But it wasn't quite closed. I got in the door. A young woman wearing a floral print dress was flipping over the closed sign at the front desk. I made it to the counter a split second before the sign flipped and put my hand next to it. Which made her look up. I gave a winning American smile. The librarian was in her twenties, strawberry blonde hair, long nose, high cheekbones, slim.

I said, "You're closing for lunch."

"Yes Monsieur."

"Can I bother you for half a minute?" I smiled.

"You can bother me for half a minute." She smiled back.

So I told her about my mother and how she had spent summers with family in town. I asked the librarian where I could look if I wanted to find traces that her family might have left.

"Your family."

"Excuse me?"

"You said you wanted to find traces of your mother's family, but it's your family as well."

Which was true, and maybe a better way of putting it. The librarian asked me to write down my mother's name and date of birth. She told me to stop by in the afternoon, say five. She said she'd see what she could dig up. But there were no guarantees. Some traces remained over time, others got wiped away. Depended on a lot of things.

I wrote the name down, *Delphine Vaugeois*, and the date of birth. Then I thanked the librarian and walked out.

Five hours. Enough time to have lunch, check out the town, take a walk, stop by the library and then get the late train out. Maybe there was a sleeper. I was headed South. Spain or Portugal and the beach. Figured I'd stay there for a month or a year, or however long it took to get bored of the beach. For the moment I was thinking about food and more coffee. Otherwise I felt good.

Off the church square, I turned into a series of narrow, crowded streets. The old town. Shoppers jostled in line for the butcher or the baker. The scent of fresh bread and coffee had settled. I squeezed through a knot of people outside the bakery and felt a push from behind. Turned to look. It was the second guy, with the leather jacket and the wet looking side part. I could smell the stuff in his hair.

So these clowns had waited for me. I had to give them points for persistence. But, what made them think I was a good mark?

Up ahead on the left was a little side street entrance, even narrower than the one I was on. I looked to the right, across the street. A new guy. Same age as rat-face, similar style. The local young thug look, but this time with longer hair in a pony tail and a manicured stubble beard. These guys were easy to spot because the rest of the crowd was older and dressed conservatively. The pony tail guy was dressed in a track suit like the rat-faced guy from the train platform.

So now there were three. The first guy with the rat-face and Adidas stripe shaved into his head, leather jacket side-part from the park, and pony tail with the facial hair.

Their plan was simple.

Leather jacket side-part was pushing up behind me so I'd move forward, out of the bakery crowd. The new guy with the pony tail was there to push me left, into the side street. I figured rat-face would be waiting there. So that was their plan. They would pen me in and try to rob me. I thought, *welcome to France*.

I stopped abruptly and let leather jacket side-part guy walk into me belly first. I felt him grab my shirt above the waist. Which was a mistake, because I used his grab to pull him closer than he wanted. I stomped on his foot with my left heel and crushed his instep. The guy grunted, surprised. The stomp made him lean forward and I whipped my right arm back and nailed him in the nuts with the heel of my hand. I pulled away from his grab and felt the back of my shirt tear as he bent over and fell.

Which pissed me off somewhat. The shirt was new.

The third guy was moving from my right, trying to corral me towards the side street. His pony tail was pulled back tight.

His little stubbly beard was carved into a thin shape on a weak face, but he had stunning bright blue eyes highlighted by dark eyelashes, like a male model. He was reaching into his pocket with his left hand, and I was on him in two steps, shutting him down. His right fist came up in a wild flail with no momentum. I stepped into the swing and at the same time transferred body weight from rear to front leg. I bent the knees, sinking low. Moved in close and punched my right elbow into his solar plexus.

The tip of the elbow made contact with a click. He went down in a sprawl.

The solar plexus is a bundle of nerves right above the abdomen, where it meets the chest. It's near impossible to actually hit the solar plexus because it sits too deep inside. But, if you get low and aim up, kind of diagonal, you can impact the nerves enough to fire off impulses to the target's diaphragm. When you get it right, the shocked nerves over-stimulate the diaphragm, which contracts. The target thinks that they are suffocating.

Which is what happened to the pony tail guy. I didn't swing my elbow in, I punched it out. The pointy part hit him right in the chest hollow. I followed through like he was made of paper. He hit the ground and started to spasm and gasp. He'd survive. In a few minutes the diaphragm would relax. But he'd get all clammy with cold sweat for at least an hour.

Two down, one to go.

I turned left to face the side street. I was right about the rat-faced guy, the number two haircut man with the Adidas stripe and small, close set eyes. He was coming out of the side street in short steps. This was someone who didn't do enough walking. Too much sitting around playing video games. I detected hesitation. His plan wasn't working out. He hadn't wanted to do it in a crowd.

He had a knife in his right hand. The blade was a Spyderco one handed opener. All steel. Pretty nasty. But the steel handle isn't much good because it gets slippery when wet. And if you're not planning on getting a knife wet, you shouldn't be taking out a knife. I stepped in quick and caught him off balance. He found himself too close-in to use the blade. I could feel the guy's breath on my face, onions and spice. He had a panicky expression, lips drawn back in a distorted scowl. People aren't generally comfortable with getting up close and personal.

I took control of his knife hand and twisted. Living beings move away from pain. So the guy tried to get away, but I kept the pressure on, pushing him back towards the side street. He groaned. His eyes rolled back in small sockets. The Spyderco clattered to the street. I adjusted my body weight and twisted quickly, pushing the trapped hand back towards the arm and up. The little scaphoid bone in his wrist snapped like a dry chopstick. He gave a little shriek.

Shouldn't have taken the knife out.

There was another high pitched shriek from my left. Which turned out to be a uniformed policewoman blowing on a whistle. We made eye contact. Hers were hazel with green flecks. She had a police cap on. Her pony tail came out the back. She had little stud earrings, made a couple of steps towards me and grabbed my shirt. "Stay there."

I relaxed and let my hands hang down, unthreatening.

ALSO BY JACK LIVELY

The Tom Keeler Novels

Straight Shot

Breacher

Enjoy this book? You can make a big difference.

Reviews are the most powerful tools in my arsenal when it comes getting attention for my books. Much as I'd like to, I don't have the financial muscle of a New York publisher. I can't take out full page ads in the newspaper or put posters on the subway.

(Not yet, anyway).

But I hope to have something much more powerful and effective than that, and it's something that those publishers would kill to get their hands on.

A committed and loyal bunch of readers.

Honest reviews of my books help bring them to the attention of other readers.

If you've enjoyed this book I would be very grateful if you could spend just five minutes leaving a review (it can be as short as you like).

Thank you very much.

JL

I hope that you have enjoyed this novella.

Consider joining my Readers Group. You'll get advanced news of new books and the occasional freebie.

Just visit the website below. Thanks for supporting me as an independent author.

-JL

jacklively.com

First Print Edition

ISBN 978-1-8380475-1-1

General Projects Ltd.

London, UK.

www.jacklively.com

Printed in Great Britain
by Amazon